Thursdays

In Savannah

For My
favorite mail lady

Olivia Gains

Also by Olivia Gaines

The Short Stories

Two Nights in Vegas
The Basemen of M. McGee
A Letter to My Mother
The Perfect Man
A New Mommy for Christmas
Beneath the Well of Dawn
The Bounty: Revenge Can be a Bitch
The Bounty: Lizzie's Vengeance

The Blakemore Files

Being Mrs. Blakemore
Shopping with Mrs. Blakemore
Dancing with Mr. Blakemore

The Novels

A Few More Nights
Friends with Benefits
The Cost To Play

Thursdays
In Savannah

Olivia Gaines

Davonshire House
Publishing

Davonshire House Publishing
PO Box 9716
Augusta, GA 30916

Copy Editor: Kathy Riehl, http://www.riehlfaithproductions.com/
Line Editor: Teresa Thompson Blackwell
Proofreader: Rachel Bishop
Special Promotions: Pilgrim Soap Company, Augusta, GA
Cover: koougraphics
Olivia Gaines Make Up and Photograph by Latasla Gardner Photography

ISBN-13: 978-0615755007
ISBN-10: 0615755003
ASIN:

Printed in the United States of America
1 2 3 4 5 6 7 10 9 8

First Davonshire House Publishing May 2014

DEDICATION

For my sister, Melanie

As a child she inspired me to read by keeping a book in my hands.

As an adult she inspires me to write by keeping my books in her hands.

Olivia Gaines

Easy reading is damn hard writing.- Nathaniel Hawthorne

ACKNOWLEDGMENTS

Thank you to my online community and network of writers.

An extra special thank you to my bibliophiles who keep my nose to the grindstone.

And thank you, for spending some time in my magical world.

Write On!

Damn, I love thursdays

Olivia Gaines

.

Prelude

Sometimes to love a man, you have to know a man. Oh, I can go back and forth all day ruminating through the argument of *does anyone ever truly know anyone?* In all honesty, you don't, you can't, and you never will. There are times in life when a man can consume you with his needs and you find yourself putting his wants, hopes, and desires before your own. Then, there are those rare occasions when you meet that man. You know the one. He's the one you make the time to love on every level.

He is that guy you hold dear to your bed, but not necessarily to your heart. Something just doesn't mesh where you can give yourself completely until that one moment when everything changes. That is when you find yourself muddling through life with Johnny Come Lately, or Johnny Comes Too Fast, only to find your better years are behind you and your baby years are staring you in the face.

I met the perfect guy. He attended the right schools, had the right job, and came from a great family. He was everything I wanted in a husband and a life partner. Over a romantic dinner at a little bistro on the outskirts of Birmingham, he took to one knee and asked me to be his. A one-carat princess cut diamond was offered to seal the deal. Amid a round of applause, followed by *oohhs* and *aahhs*, I consented to be Mrs. Darwin Finney.

Life was grand. I would have my Mercedes, two point three children, an expensive dog, soccer practice with little Jr., and dance recitals with the little princess. I was on my way, but I made one pit stop.

Jesse Orison. That man made me lose my freaking mind! He was the wrong guy at the wrong time and in the wrong damn place. That place was my bed, almost every Thursday night. Well, loose interpretation, I invited him in the front door and into my bed. The problem was, once he came inside, he made no plans to leave. I had a busy week so I asked him to come over on a Thursday. I know, but he scheduled himself for every Thursday and I cleared my calendar to make room for him and dear heavens, I turned into a lovesick fool.

There, are you satisfied?

Anyhoo ... I was engaged to be married. I was not a loose woman. But that damned Jesse.... When we got behind closed doors....

Hi. I am Savannah Niden and I am in trouble. I need someone to hear me out, not judge my actions or choices. Just hear me out. The wedding is in a month and I am not certain if I want to marry for stability or marry the man who makes me happy. Maybe getting some of this off my chest will help me figure out what to do. I hope you are ready for an earful.

Chapter One

February 14th

Soft music played in the background as Darwin Finney escorted his date into the five star restaurant. Tonight was going to be a special evening and everything was set. The champagne had been pre-ordered, the chef had been notified, and the musicians were ready. Darwin was dressed in his best black suit, a fresh haircut, clean-shaven, and sporting his favorite cologne. He arrived at the bistro with a game plan. It was true what many said about the two. They were indeed a striking couple, but looks were so often deceiving.

Savannah Niden, PhD. was the total package. She was the perfect woman to adorn his arm as he made his way toward senior partner in his architecture firm. The only things left were the formalities of an engagement ring, followed by the betrothal party, a tea at the country club, and a year to plan the wedding. During the year Mrs. Finney, his mother, would introduce her in all the right social circles. Savannah would make new friends, pick out a nice home in Vestavia Hills, and within the next two years, give him a son. In return, she would have a household expense account, a new Mercedes every three years, a large closet, and two perfect children, along with a non-shedding dog.

Savannah and Darwin had been together for a year and a half. The lady understood what this night was about and was ready to receive the blessings. She smiled when the champagne was brought to the table and uncorked. She placed her hand on her chest as the cork popped and she feigned surprise. There was even a practiced giggle that escaped her lips as she sipped the bubbly. The truth was she hated champagne. She also hated this stuffy ass restaurant. The Chef never got an order right, even if you requested a grilled chicken breast.

Savannah had ordered the lamb chops, partly to piss off Darwin and ruin his perfect evening, but mostly because she had lost her appetite. True to form, when Chef Robens sent out the meal, the lamb chops were still bleeding, the potatoes were cold and the asparagus was limp. She nibbled on a roll that must have been on the shelf too long and been reheated.

"What is the matter, Love? Don't you like your meal?" Darwin asked as he watched her push food around her plate.

"The chops are a bit too rare," she told him as she sipped on her champagne.

"It befuddles me why you always order something you've never tried or don't understand and then seem disappointed when it arrives," he told her as he cut a large chunk from his bloody steak.

In a nutshell, the same could be said for their relationship. Hunger is a good teacher. Once you have been there, it is the one place a person never wants to revisit. Savannah smiled a coy smile. "I know. I am trying to expand my palate, but bloody meat is not my thing."

"Next time order something simple, something you know you like, maybe some chicken or something." He spoke to her as if she were a child incapable of making a decision. Instead of responding with something snappish or a chiding remark, she sat in silence, watching him masticate a large chunk of cow with his oversized teeth and wondered if their children would have a big head like he did. He wasn't an unattractive man; he was just average.

That was the thing about Darwin. He was simply mediocre. He was of normal height and regular build. He made a six-figure income, which was usual for his business, but his salary was low for the number of years he had been in his field. He was a fair kisser, a moderate thinker, and hovered around boring in bed. There were things he was very good at doing.

Patronizing her was at the top of the list, followed by a kind heart, a positive spirit, an optimistic outlook on life, and his unabated love for her. In his eyes, she could do no wrong and Savannah worked hard not to disappoint him. He was, after all, the key to her cushy future.

Her hand flew to her chest when he pulled out the Tiffany blue box. Tears flooded her eyes when he opened the token of love to reveal the one-carat princess cut diamond, flanked with a tapered band. Darwin even added two topaz stones, which cast a golden hue on the brilliance of the diamond. Her excitement was not holstered when he got down on one knee and asked for her hand in marriage.

She accepted with tears of joy and pecked at his face with kisses. Diners in the restaurant applauded as she held up her hand to show off her new present. She had arrived. Savannah belonged to someone who was happy to have her. The days of going to bed hungry had long since been over, but in her mind, she was always one paycheck away from being back in that unfortunate spot. Darwin was her ticket to make sure that didn't happen to her ever again. Her consent to marriage was based mainly on two simple thoughts: being poor was no fun and being hungry was even worse.

They chatted amicably about the engagement party in April. He told her about the tea at the country club in May. There would be dress shopping in New York in June, something in July, and blah, blah, blah in August. She heard little of what he said after that. She only knew the wedding was this time next year, on Valentine's Day. It was corny, but she would go along with it.

His phone chirped, which meant he had to leave. Her car was close by so she would make her way downtown to her condo. She truly loved it, because she had scrimped and saved to make the down payment herself. She had a few bucks in the bank, but not nearly enough to make her feel secure. Savannah was always skimping and scraping to get the bills paid. Pride filled her, as she was always grateful to pay her own mortgage. She was content with driving her ten-year-old Ford, but damn, she sure would look good in a Mercedes. It was a fair trade, an accomplished wife living an accomplished life. It mattered little that her betrothed was as exciting as watching fecal matter dry on a wall. Darwin gave her a quick kiss on her cheek as he settled the tab and ran off for whatever emergency was calling him. She wouldn't be surprised if it were revealed that her soon to be husband was having a last minute love fest with some dumb, weave-wearing woman that liked to twerk in his lap, but she didn't care. The end and the means were all justified.

After Darwin's departure, she sent back the chops and

ordered a salad. She grazed on it until she was hit with a genius idea. She would head to a local hotspot and have a drink before heading home. Savannah hoped she would get lucky and find someone she could have a good conversation with. Maybe they could talk about a book or an upcoming vacation. *Lord knows I could use some change in my life.*

Chapter Two

The club was loud and the patrons were rowdy, but it seemed like the perfect place to have a bit of fun. It wasn't every day that a girl got engaged and she wanted to celebrate. A few people from her complex were here tonight. She waved at one and danced with another. She made eye contact with someone who looked like a guy from her speech class at the University of Alabama at Birmingham, some years prior when she was completing her undergraduate work.

Oh crap. She had made eye contact for too long and he was on his way over. *What was his name?*

"Savannah Niden, is that you?" he asked as he leaned in to kiss her cheek. His breath reeked of scotch, and he had a bad tooth. Both smelled sour.

"Greg, right? We had speech together at UAB?"

"It was more classes than just speech." He helped himself to a seat. She continued looking toward the door, hoping somebody, anybody, would see her in distress and rescue her from the man who thought she was the one who got away.

"You know, I was a little obsessed with you in college." He smiled at her through drunken eyes. His coffee-colored skin had an ashen hue, symbolizing the presence of sickness. "I admit, I'm still a little taken with you. You are such a fine specimen of a woman," he added through slobbering words.

She placed her hand on his to show off her new ring.

"That is so sweet of you. I am engaged, but it was good running into you." As she stood up, he grabbed her roughly by the arm and forced her back into the seat.

"Back then, you treated me like I wasn't good enough for you. But I'll be damned if I let you do it to me now!"

It was a reflex action. Savannah grabbed his pinky finger and began twisting until he let go. "You were always overly aggressive Greg, with way too much to prove." She continued pushing the finger until he relaxed his grip on her arm. "Again, it was good seeing you." She placed a ten on the counter to cover her drink. "Have a good night."

Savannah was nearly out of breath as she slid into the driver's seat of her car. She locked the doors and checked the rear view mirror. It was too late to argue with herself for not following her instincts to head for the door when she spotted Greg. Something about him always made her uneasy. She started the car and checked for traffic before she pulled out and headed home.

The bar was only a few blocks from the condo community where she resided. She pulled into the parking structure to find that someone had blocked her space. She circled around and the only available space was in the very dark far corner. *Fine.* Saying a silent prayer, she pulled into the slot. Her suspicious nature made her check the rear and side view mirrors. She pulled out her flashlight from the glove box and her pepper spray from her bag, and then opened the driver's side door.

Instantly, she felt hands around her throat as she was yanked forward and slammed onto the hood of her car. She fought back as her assailant threw her against the wall, tearing her clothing. She felt the skin rip on her shoulder blade as he slid her side to side against the rough bricks on the wall. "Don't scream bitch or I'll gut you!" Savannah felt the knife press against her breast and she screamed anyway.

"If you're going to gut me, then do it now, because in a minute, I'm going to fuck you up!" The assailant was shocked. The self-defense course she had taken taught her to fight back and this man was in for a rude awakening. It was all the time she needed. She followed up her threat with pepper spray to his eyes and mouth, a knee to his groin, a small, but powerful right fist to his chin, and then one more kick in his nuts for good measure. She stood over him, looking down and screaming at the top of her lungs, "Fire, fire, fire, you sorry son of a biscuit maker!" She screamed again and again until she heard footsteps on the stairwell as a burly white man, wearing a tool belt ran into the parking structure.

"Miss, are you okay?"

"Do I look like I'm okay, Einstein?"

The silk cream-colored blouse she was wearing was torn, there was a small knick from the tip of the assailant's blade on her breast and the skin had been scraped from her back where he threw her against the brick wall. Savannah wished she had put on her jacket. "This fool attacked me," she yelled as she kicked him again and sprayed his face with more pepper spray, and then she insulted his manhood.

Tool belt guy leaned down to check the attacker. As he turned him over, he asked, "Do you know this man?"

Oh my goodness, it's Greg! He had followed her home. But wait, he knew which parking space was hers. *Dear*

God, he has been watching me!

"Vaguely," she muttered.

"Do you want me to call the police?"

She looked at Greg, who was now struggling to get to his feet. "Greg. Do I need to call the police? Or have you had enough?" She sprayed him in the mouth with more pepper spray, as the tool belt-wearing rescuer snatched the container from her hand.

She eyed his profile with some annoyance until he turned and looked at her head on. Savannah lost her train of thought. The man had muscles on top of muscles, stood at least six feet tall, a head full of jet black hair, clear piercing blue eyes, and a little over a five o'clock shadow, and he had just stolen her breath. When those blue eyes locked with her brown ones, the stumbling Greg was nearly forgotten. Well, that was until Greg swung blindly, catching her rescuer off guard and cold-cocking him on the nose.

Tool belt guy raised the pepper spray and sprayed Greg again, making him scream, "Son of a bitch!"

"Take your silly ass home Greg, and stop acting like a darn fool. If I ever see you anywhere near me again, I swear I'll shoot you!" She took out her camera phone, snapped photos of him and tool belt guy's nose, and then handed the phone to her bleeding helper who was trying to stop the blood flow, but managed to snap a photo of her condition. In her purse was her favorite handkerchief, which she retrieved quickly to apply to Mr. Handy's nose to help stop the bleeding. They were a sight. His shirt was now covered in blood, her clothing was torn, her back was bleeding and the nearly blind Greg was stumbling about the parking lot. She kicked him in the butt again, just for good measure.

She didn't know what made her do what happened next. Looking back on it, she probably shouldn't have, but she was a helpful person.

"Come on, I'll help you clean up, if you help put something on my back." He was going to need ice and fast, if not, he would have two black eyes in the morning. She took him by the arm and led him to the elevator as he held his head back. Savannah steered the stranger, who had way too much sex appeal, toward the front door of her condo.

Looking back, she realized too late that her first error was letting him in the door.

Chapter Three

The ride to the third floor was quick. Each floor only held three condo units with an upstairs and downstairs. She unlocked the front door and led him to the downstairs bathroom. It only took a minute for her to grab a washcloth and head to the kitchen to load it with ice. When she returned to the bathroom, she found him sitting on the toilet with the lid down, cursing under his breath.

"Thank you for helping me," she told him as she pressed the ice to his nose. "My name is Savannah."

He extended a calloused upside down left hand, "I'm Jesse Orison." His right hand was still covering his nose.

"I've seen you around the building. Are you the super or something?"

Jesse was attempting to get his bearings while trying to look at the pretty woman and stop the blood flow from his nose that was rushing to his pants, "Something like that."

His shirt was covered in blood from his nose, which did not seem to want to stop bleeding. She remembered that she had an extra-large tee that her brother had left there and she ran to fetch it. When she returned, Jesse had removed his bloody shirt and tool belt so he could wash his face in the sink. His body was magnificent. It was easy to see that those climbing, winding, well-defined muscles were earned from hard work, versus carbo-loading and pumping iron in the gym. She lowered her eyes, ashamed that she had just gotten engaged less than an hour ago, and was now thinking unladylike thoughts about this stranger.

She could smell the sweat on him.

He smelled like a man who worked hard for a living.

She also smelled the angst.

He was reacting like a man in need of a woman's care and attention.

The tension between the two of them was palpable. The pheromones he had deposited in that small space ignited something in her. Savannah wanted him with a fierceness she had never experienced. Leaning against the door jamb, taking in all of the awesomeness of Jesse Orison, a fleeting thought crossed her mind.... *What if?*

"I brought a first aid kit back as well," she told him as she sat it on the counter. Jesse checked the contents and found some gauze and antibacterial ointment. Without warning, his massive paw encircled her forearm and pulled her into the bathroom and attempted to turn her to face the mirror. His nose hadn't completely stopped bleeding, so Savannah turned back around and removed an applicator-less tampon from the first aid kit and shoved it up his nostril. His grip was firm as he turned her again to face the mirror, his man parts just inches away from her hips, radiating heat and beckoning her girl parts to join him for a party. Jesse's careful hands slid her blouse off her shoulders, easing it away from the skin and fabric that had begun to stick to the scrapes and bits of torn flesh.

"It's not too deep," he said in a deep voice as he washed the affected area with a cotton ball, applied the salve, and then the bandage. Two pats to her collarbones and he took a step back. "There you go, all better." She intentionally turned around slowly, allowing curious fingers to graze his midsection. As Jesse reached for the shirt she had brought him, she reached for his hands, interlacing her fingers within his own. Her ring scraped his fingers and he stepped back even further.

"I don't dig in another man's garden. I'm sorry." He started to pull on the tee, raising it over his head, and Savannah became the aggressor.

Before he could get the shirt on, she grabbed the fabric, trapping his hands and blinding him. "What if the gardener hasn't weeded in a while?" Savannah hopped onto the bathroom counter, pulling Jesse closer so he could feel the heat that was rising from her body. Her mouth touched the skin on his chest. Jesse jumped back as if he had been burned. Her fingers trailed across the broad expanse of his pectorals as she held him captive with her other hand. Pulling the fabric forward, he moved with it so their mouths were only inches apart.

"Jesse, I believe in staying in my own backyard, but there are times when you need to sink your toes in a new piece of real estate." Her tongue ran across his bottom lip, causing his breath to catch.

Although he couldn't see her through the cotton fabric, her scent permeated his nostrils, sending signals to his male parts to wake up. It was go time. "Is that your plan, to borrow me for a few hours?"

"If that is okay with you. I promise not to hurt you." She licked his top lip.

"What if I don't make that promise?" He leaned forward and kissed her lightly.

"I don't need your assurances, Jesse Orison, I need your body." She released the shirt by yanking it over his eyes.

"I can't," he told her, grabbing for his shirt. "I am not prepared and you are not in your right mind."

It took her a minute to understand what he was saying as he backed away. Within seconds, he slipped the tee over his head, put his tool belt back on and handed her a business card, a simple one with his name and phone number on yellow card stock.. Nothing else.

Savannah looked at the card like it was a complex math problem. "What am I supposed to do with this?"

Jesse took her face into his hands and kissed her lightly on the lips. "You have had an intense evening, with the attack and all. If you are serious and you want to be with me, here's my number. Call me in a week."

"And if I choose not to?" she asked as she stuck his card in the first aid kit.

"Then ..." he smiled as he tightened his tool belt. "... my lovely lady, it was a pleasure to meet you."

Savannah was still sitting on the countertop in her bra looking confused. This man was actually going to walk away from her and leave her like this, all worked up with no man to ride. Quickly bounding to her feet, she stood in the bathroom door, staring at him in disbelief.

"You have the number," he told her as he looked back at her one last time before he walked out the door.

It was a sorry Thursday and an even worse Valentine's Day.

Savannah wasn't certain why she didn't mention the incident in the parking garage to Darwin, her mother, or any of her friends. Over the next few days, she kept a close eye on where she parked and tried to check and see if anyone was watching her. Thus far, it had been an uneventful week.

Darwin came over for dinner on Tuesday night. She couldn't remember anything that they had spoken about or any high points of their conversation. He claimed he didn't care for her bed and refused to make love to her in the condo that he also felt was too small. Once, when he had been feeling a tad bit randy, they went at it on the couch. By the time she was warmed up and ready to cut loose, he was finished and was urging her to hurry up. It had been a year and a half of average sex. She really needed something more than her friend in the nightstand drawer.

On Thursday evening, she had stopped for Chinese takeout and a new magazine and was anxiously awaiting her soft fluffy couch that had been calling her. She called Darwin to see if he wanted to come over, but he was busy. Next she called her girlfriend Sheryl, but she was tied up, literally. Oh well, this wasn't the first night she'd been alone. She grabbed a plate from the cabinet and noticed the first aid kit sitting on the kitchen counter. She opened it.

Jesse's card was sitting on top.

Savannah stared at the card.

The card stared back.

Savannah's eyes wandered over to look at her phone.

The phone said, "Do it!"

One last look back at the card, which appeared to have moved closer to the phone, forcing her by a string of cosmic gamma rays she swore, had taken over her will power. She picked up the phone and punched in the number. He answered on the third ring.

"This is Jesse."

"Jesse, this is Savannah Niden."

He was quiet.

"From last week," she said as she bit her lip.

"Ah, Savannah, how are you?"

"I am well, thank you for asking."

She was quiet.

So was he.

"Well, it has been a week and I'm calling."

"Okay," was all he said.

Who did he think he was? She didn't have time for games, plus he knew why she was calling. "Are you coming over or not?"

"I'll be there in 20 minutes." With that, he hung up the phone.

Savannah was making her second mistake. She had called to invite him back inside.

Thursdays in Savannah

Chapter Four

Savannah checked her watch. It was five thirty. There was no time for a shower, but she rushed to her bathroom, freshened up, and brushed her teeth. She ran into her bedroom, changed her underwear, and turned back the bed. Although she had already removed her work clothes, she checked her legs to make sure they didn't need a quick razor run over them before she slipped on a sexy black skirt and a bit of a high heeled shoe. High heels always made her feel sexy. At five fifty-five, her doorbell rang.

She opened the door to find Jesse standing there with his tool belt hanging on his hip, a formerly red metal toolbox in one hand, and a small black gym bag in the other. She opened the door wider to allow him entrance. *He brought a toolbox ... thoughtful.* The grey carpenter pants he wore showed the definition of strong thighs, and the polo shirt with an emblem of Montgomery Construction clung to all the muscles she would be gripping as she rode him to her happy place in orgasm heaven. The other item he wore was a smile that moistened her underwear.

"Hey, you," he said as he closed and locked the door. He put down his toolbox, which clanked with the sound of his tools settling into compartments. He removed his tool belt and took off his steel toe grey boots. Savannah's mind was on his tools. As he up righted himself, she heard a loud grumbling.

"Hey back!" She watched him closely. "Was that your

stomach growling?"

"Yeah, I haven't had much time to eat. It's been a bit hectic today."

"I ordered some Chinese takeout and have more than enough. Wash up and join me in the kitchen for dinner."

Savannah wasn't sure what she was doing, but her mama taught her *Man Care 101*: feed him first, then love him and let him sleep. As he washed his hands in the downstairs bathroom, she set out the food, two glasses of sweetened ice tea, two forks, two knives, and for a little flare, her good cloth napkins. *Ah hell, why not*? The iPod was cued up to some soft jazz and she lit a candle on the table.

Jesse came to the table and eyed the food and soft candlelight, and listened to the music, all while trying to disguise the large smile threatening to take over his face. "This looks amazing. Intimate and quaint. Thank you." He took a seat and asked her to bow her head as he blessed the food. Just as she had been taught, Savannah stood next to the man, allowing her thigh to touch his arm as she fixed him a plate then made her own.

The man was full of surprises, as he did nothing crass like run his hands up her skirt or feel her butt, yet none of his actions resonated as much as a modest question he asked her before digging into the food. "How has your week been?"

Simple as that, a conversation was started. She told him she worked at the University in the research lab. The conversation then changed to his job and he mentioned an outdoor kitchen that was being added to one of the first floor models in the building, one that he had been assigned to oversee. After dinner was finished, Jesse collected the plates, washed the dishes, and placed them in the rack to drain.

Blue eyes bore into her, taking in her lips and caressing her body, but never in a manner that was vulgar or suggestive. "Can I get a washcloth and towel? I need to get some of the day off me."

"You want to take a shower?"

"If you want it dirty, I can do that too, but I would feel much sexier if I were clean," he told her with a very serious expression. A sly smile crept across his face as he stared deeply into her eyes, sending goose bumps up and down her arms. That look was the first sign he had given her that he planned to work her over.

A few moments later, she returned with a green hand towel and a pink washcloth. Jesse looked at both with some confusion as neither was large enough for him to towel dry nor cover any chunk of body part.

"I'll do the rest." Her eyes grazed up and down his body, coming back to his face, accepting the challenge he had silently issued earlier. Savannah planned to give back as good as he gave.

Jesse grabbed the small bag by the door, removing the clean tee she had loaned him. He was familiar with the units in the complex so he knew where the second guest bathroom was and made his way up the stairs. She could hear the shower and listened as the sound changed from water hitting the cold tile to water hitting his hot body. The sound of his whistling made her think of his lips. The sheer concept of him soaping up sent her mind into overdrive and then it shifted gears to her sex drive. Both were revving up for a steamy evening. Lost in her thoughts, she didn't hear the turning of the taps and the cessation of the water.

"Savannah," he said in a low voice from the top of the stairs.

She heard him call her name as she walked to the foot of the stairwell, looking upwards to see him standing there, the hand towel purposefully placed in front of him while water was still beading on his sun tanned skin. Slowly she climbed the steps. As her right foot hit the bottom stair, her skirt swished and she unbuttoned the first button of her blouse. With each step she undid another button, as if doing a stair-climbing strip tease until she finally reached the top of the stairwell. Her blouse was open, her chest was heaving, and her body was tingling. Jesse dropped the hand towel and pulled her in close to his wet body.

"If you hadn't called, I would have come back anyway to return the shirt." He smiled at her as he pressed his maleness against her body.

Her arms slipped around his neck, her fingers toying with the wet strands of his hair. "So, I guess that means you have been thinking about me."

He almost growled the words as his lips pressed against her neck, kissing, nibbling, and inhaling her essence, "All damned week long, Savannah. I barely got anything done."

"What were you thinking?" she asked as she leaned in and ran her tongue across his bottom lip like she had before.

"I would rather just show you." He lowered his head, bringing his mouth to her lips. There was no resistance. Her lips parted to accept his tongue as he lifted her from the floor and carried her to the bedroom. He lowered her to the bed, bracing his weight on his forearms.

"Savannah, I am pretty strong, but I will try to be gentle." He didn't want to tell her how busy he had been in the past few months, leaving little if no time for what they were about to do. As his stomach had growled earlier indicating his hunger, his body was close to the same. He was hungry for her touch and her desire to love him. The whiskers from his beard tickled her, making contact with her skin as his kisses went down her neck to her breasts, and he massaged the mounds harnessed inside her bra. He released the prisoners, exposing the nipples, not even bothering to unfasten the brassiere.

"Don't be," she whispered as she pulled at his hair, then running her hands over his broad shoulders.

He pulled back and stood up. He was magnificent. "I will give you one last chance to change your mind. I don't want to deal with your regrets later."

"I'm not changing it." She removed her blouse and unfastened her bra, which had been pulled down under her breasts. She made a futile attempt to kick off her shoes and remove the skirt, but she only managed to half-accomplish either task.

"Take off that ring when you are in bed with me," he told her.

Savannah was so far gone in her need, she didn't care that his words implied this would not be their only time together. Jesse pulled three condoms from his bag, some Astroglide, and a can of whipped cream. Her eyes got wide as she snatched the lubricant from his hands and threw it across the room. Jesse only shrugged and laughed as she crawled back onto the bed.

The only thing that came to Savannah's mind was that

Jesse must be a helluva handyman because his hands were magical. He used his fingers, his mouth, and every tool at his resource to warm her up. When she could no longer take the teasing, he applied the protection and poised himself for entry.

It had been a long time since he had been this turned on by a woman. The need to have her consumed his every thought. All he wanted was to be inside of her, but the hesitation that held him back was that he had not even coupled with her and knew he would want more. "This is fricking crazy, you know that right?" He kissed her again, applying a bit of pressure with his hips.

"I don't care, all I know is how badly I need you. I can't wait to feel you inside of me, Jesse," she mumbled as her anxious hands roamed over his back, sinking her nails into the flesh, encouraging him to connect their bodies.

"Not as badly as I need you." He grabbed her hand and pushed it down to where their bodies were about to be joined. "Can you feel that? That is prom night hard."

Everything about Jesse was big and once her hand touched where he instructed, Savannah's eyes closed as she drifted away into a quiet world where only the two of them would exist. "Look at me," he growled at her. She lifted her heavy head out of the soft pillows, looked up with her brown eyes met the stinging intensity of his irises, which were now a brilliant cerulean blue. He slipped a pillow under her hips as he leaned forward, to kiss her and thrust himself into her. Savannah's breath caught in her throat, as he held her gaze. She felt so full of Jesse.

He pulled back slightly and pushed, more gently this time, into her again whispering, "Damn, that is a snug fit and you feel so good." He buried his head in her shoulder and began to work his hips incrementally as he inserted himself farther into her. Jesse's lips connected again with her own as he raised her thigh to gain deeper access. He felt her body tense up and watched her face as she winced. "Is it painful for you?" he asked.

"Yes, a little bit," she mumbled into the thickness of his shoulder. "But I like it.... I like it a lot." She moved cautiously, providing timid movements with her hips, but her eyes were telling him something more. Jesse shifted himself and took a few minutes to allow her body to adjust to his invasion.

"You're holding back, Savannah. Let go, let me feel you enjoying me," he whispered in her ear, along with a few things that seem to loosen her reserve. She followed his instructions as goose bumps grew up and down her arms again. She rolled her right hip upwards and thrust it at him. Jesse moaned. The same action was followed with her left hip and he called to the Holy Trinity, closing his eyes. She locked her legs around his hips and rolled him to his back as all the tension began to leave her body. She moved her hips to work him all in, relishing the feeling of him inside of her. The thickness of him pressed against her walls, his length filling her up and stroking her from the inside, which brought an increase in her movements. Her desire peaked and she needed all of him at once. His eyes were closed.

"Look at me," she whispered as the freedom to express herself sexually was unlocked and she let go. She began slowly at first, riding him like a bar bull, gradually rocking forward, lifting, and rocking back. These actions were repeated over and over as she stared into his eyes.

His calloused hands held her hips, the rough skin of his palms moving up and down her flesh, encouraging her to move as she needed.

"Jesse." She whispered his name as she felt her passion building. It wasn't enough. She needed extra movement from him. "Give me more, Jesse, I need more."

Before she knew it, she was face down on the bed and he was behind her. The pillow was under her stomach as he worked, thrust, and worked her some more. He used long strokes as his lower abdomen slapped against her hips, his givers of life hitting her low. In minutes she was at her climax and he pulled away.

"Not yet, my lovely, but soon."

Jesse kissed her shoulders and rolled her to her back. Sweat soaked and breathing heavily, she reached for him, silently pleading for him to end the sweet suffering. He grabbed the can of whipped cream and sprayed a foamy circle on each of her nipples. Leisurely and rhythmically, his fingers tortured her, his thumb massaging the queen in the tower. He licked the whipped cream from her nipples; she was so close. Without warning, he plunged back into her, allowing his fingers to continue to work as she bucked her hips furiously against him. Her hands beat on his chest and she let go, screaming his name as tears began pouring from her eyes. He was still working her as he reached his climax, trying to catch his own breath, thrusting hard, gritting his teeth. Jesse's powerful body was pushing, thrusting, and pumping himself into her as the woman in her clamped around him, milking him. Their bodies collapsed in a heap of sweat, arms and legs entangled as they both breathed hard. He spoke only one word as he wiped away the cleansing tears streaming down her face, "Damn." He held her close, breathing in her spirit, unable to voice what he was feeling. Her tears were indicative of how repressed she had been sexually and letting go was the start of something new for Savannah.

Jesse extricated himself and went to the bathroom to flush the waste. Savannah pulled back the bed covers to welcome him into her bed when he returned. He leaned back into the pillows and pulled her by the arm to lie on his chest. Her skirt was still on, but twisted. He hadn't bothered to remove her underwear, which was now giving her an evil wedgie, while one shoe still dangled from her foot. Savannah Niden had experienced something for the first time in her life: sexual satisfaction.

She had to keep this to herself. Savannah made a mental decision to close the door to the outside world. While she was here with Jesse, she would allow herself to be free. She had a year before she walked down the aisle. One year to be with Jesse – that is if he was willing to share these stolen moments.

The evening ended in a darkened room with two bodies moving against each other in the wee hours of the morning. Jesse whispered her name as he claimed her body, teaching it to respond to his touch. Savannah wasn't going to take the risk of never again experiencing the intensity of what they had shared. Once more would not make a difference now. She had already cheated. She may as well enjoy herself.

The alarm sounded at six am. A sore, weary, and

cheerful Savannah made breakfast consisting of egg white omelets with spinach and Swiss cheese. When she packed her lunch of a turkey breast sandwich on wheat, a container of Progresso soup, and an apple, she packed a brown bag for the maintenance man as well. Jesse slowly descended the stairs, wearing black carpenter pants and a blue Montgomery Construction shirt. His eyes were droopy, but not red-rimmed as he yawned like a big bear waking up from hibernation. *Hmmmm, he brought a change of clothing.*

"Good morning," he said as he walked up behind her, enveloped her in his arms, and placed a kiss on her jaw line.

"Did you sleep okay, Jesse?" she asked as she placed a plate on the table for him.

"I slept when you allowed me to." He kissed her lightly on the lips. "You are indeed an exceptional lover." He sampled the omelet. "And a good cook, too."

After a quick blessing of the food, they dug into breakfast. No words were spoken, just smiles across the table at the other, remembering the passionate night they had shared. After Jesse washed the dishes, he squatted by the door, donning his work boots. Savannah handed him a brown bag with the two sandwiches and an apple. "Your lunch for today." It may have been too much, but she was thankful for the evening they shared. She always heeded Mama's Rules of Man Care: make him feel cared for.

Jesse stared at the brown paper bag. *She made me lunch.* He pulled her in for another kiss. "A man could get used to this because you are indeed something special, Savannah Niden."

The one thing that was lacking with Darwin was

honesty, especially when it came to what she wanted and needed to say. If Jesse was going to be a part of her life, in whatever fashion, they would have to start out with truthfulness. As she faced him, his hands caressed her arms, her left hand resting across his heart while she spoke to him. "Last night, you were everything I had hoped, more than I expected, and exactly what I needed." She gave him a squeeze and stepped back.

With his tool belt on, boots laced, and lunch stuck in his toolbox, Jesse leaned against the door jamb looking back at her. Words bounced around in his head like ping-pong balls springing against what he was feeling, thinking, and wanting. Adding to the uncertainty of his actions in *tilling another man's soil*, he wasn't quite sure what to say since he wanted more of her, so he said the first thing that came to mind, "Tinkerbell."

Savannah furrowed her brow trying to connect his words to a fairy tale creature. He walked over to her and slipped his arms about her waist.

A light kiss was planted on the side of her face before he spoke. "When I was 17, my dad gave me a Camaro. I had it refinished and had yellow and red flames painted down the nose fading into the sleek body."

"Every time I slid inside of her, I gave her a few gentle touches and she would come alive under me. No matter how hard I pushed her, she responded, giving me everything she had."

He licked his index finger and touched her right nipple, which hardened at his touch. "Her gears were so smooth, all it took was a finger or two to get her revved up and man, once she warmed up it was like flying on the wind. The connection between us was unlike anything I had ever experienced."

He paused and looked into her eyes, the crystal blue turning cerulean as he licked his bottom lip. "That is, until now."

Savannah swallowed hard, gulping back the rising emotions in her voice and the swirl of feelings in her pants. "I take it you named her Tinkerbell?"

He kissed her hard on the mouth, reluctantly letting go. "You have the number." That was all he said, as he again walked out her front door.

Savannah stared at the entrance, filled with dread, impure thoughts and a terrible knowledge that she had made her third and final mistake. She let Jesse Orison into her bed, and he liked it. The real problem was so did she and her body was looking forward to the next encounter.

Chapter Five

Friday was a very quiet day. Savannah smiled to herself as she ran test tubes through the centrifuge. Remembering Jesse's soft words in her ear as he encouraged her to let go sent a rush of feelings through her body and butterflies to her stomach. It was hard to feel guilty about doing something wrong, when something so wrong felt so good.

Her mother called at lunchtime to schedule a shopping date for Saturday morning. Savannah was uncertain why she agreed, but it was her mother and she needed to focus on something other than the man who was in her bed last night. Tonight, she would head to Sheryl's for book club and Saturday night, it would be dinner at Darwin's with his parents.

Nice and orderly, just as it should be.

Friday Night

Her mind wandered all during book club and she found herself daydreaming and smiling at the most inopportune moments. Her friends and fellow bibliophiles fancied she was wandering off into the land of bridal gowns and intricately embroidered veils. The group was reading *Hard Lessons* by Ruth P. Watson, which made Savannah frown a bit. This whole situation with Jesse was going to be a hard lesson, but life was too short and so was her engagement.

Order was for chumps and she wanted to feel alive, if only for a moment.

Saturday Morning

Emurial Niden could almost smell another man on her daughter's skin. "I hope he's worth losing everything you have worked so hard to obtain." Savannah pretended to be shocked, appalled, and offended at her mother's words. With a twist of her lips and a roll of her eyes, her mother quickly let her know she wasn't buying it, especially after she saw her daughter buy something skimpy and sexy at Victoria's Secret.

Emurial was full of skepticism and asked her daughter, with some reservations, "You think Darwin will like that in red?"

"I'm not certain, Mama, but I can only try."

An attempt with Darwin was all that Savannah ever made since her fiancé was not an adventurous type of man. If he liked something, he wanted the same thing all the time. If he hated it, he never wanted to see it again. When they made love, he liked her on the bottom, with absolutely no deviations. If he liked the red outfit, he would want her to wear it every time they made love. As she told her mother, *I can only try*.

Saturday Night

Trying was the perfect word on Saturday evening. Darwin's mother sat around making snarky comments about Savannah's favorite blue dress, saying it made her skin tone look sickly. Ann Marie Finney was not a woman to be trifled with. Social reputations lived and died at her word. "That color is all wrong for your skin tone dear. A

35

warm complexioned woman should dress like a red-head, in pinks and lavenders, to make her skin shimmer."

Savannah's tight smile was frozen on her face, telling her future mother-in-law that she would make a note to never wear this dress to any function with these people, but it was one of her favorite dresses and she was keeping it. Dinner was stiff and the conversation was dull, but the food was digestible. Darwin's father sat there like a dark lump of bituminous coal, ready to be used, but not quite enough quality to burn hot. Everything on the dinner plate was like Darwin's dad. It could have used more panache, some flavor, and a touch of wow.

The first chair violinist at the Alabama Symphony Orchestra was one of the dinner guests. She played beautifully as the family sat with half-filled glasses of wine for an impromptu private concert. Closed eyes savored each well-played note while heads bobbed and weaved as if the melodic tunes were floating the small audience away on clouds of merriment and hope. To Savannah, they looked like well-coiffed cobras being charmed by the pungi. The audience provided a round of applause before members of the small group disbanded, saying their good nights and wishing the other attendees well.

It was a quick drive over the hill to Darwin's home, where Savannah revealed her sexy surprise for the evening. He hated the red lingerie, saying it made her look cheap, and asked her to remove it. She returned to the bed in a white cotton nightgown and returned his kisses that were too wet, as she tried to accept his entry into her body, which was not nearly wet enough. Darwin made a bumbled attempt at foreplay, but soon her mind wandered to Jesse, which shifted her into high gear.

She became aggressive and Darwin's eagerness to have her dwindled, forcing an apology on her part. "You got me so worked up Darwin. I don't know what came over me." He accepted her apology and four minutes later, she lay there, smiling in the dark, telling him lies that he made her feel good, but she was not dishonest with her words when she told him she was lucky to have him in her life.

Sunday Morning

Darwin and Savannah attended church service, put something in the collection plate, and headed to her mother's for Sunday dinner. A nice, simple pot roast with vegetables, a green salad and crusty rolls seemed like a five course dinner after last night's dry rubbed meat and stiff mashed potatoes.

"I am so pleased that Savannah inherited your cooking skills, Mrs. Niden," Darwin complimented her mother. On the way home, he would complain that the food was too salty and would probably make him swell up.

"It is the reason why so many of our people are riddled with high blood pressure, diabetes, and gout," he told her as if she did not research those diseases for a living.

Savannah packed a doggy bag so she could have a bit more for supper later and use some of the meat tomorrow for lunch. A couple of flour tortillas and she would have soft tacos for her mid-day meal. Nothing was ever wasted with her. Everything had to count.

The start of the workweek was daunting as Savannah hit a few snags. Vials had been improperly labeled, causing the wrong batches to be sampled, and she would have to start Phase IV of the research all over again. Explaining this to her boss only exacerbated the frustration in her week. By Wednesday, she was tense and experiencing a major migraine, and ready to end a few people's lives. As an assistant professor at the University, she taught a few courses each quarter, but her strength was in the research portions and grant writing. It was the livelihood of her department and it was up to her to keep everything on track and on budget. If there was one thing she knew better than all others, it was how to maintain a budget.

On Thursday, she had everything back on trajectory and had to write up her lab tech for a poor job performance that had caused the setbacks. She arrived home at a quarter of five with two steaks, a head of butter leaf lettuce and some artesian dinner rolls. The phone somehow magically appeared in her hand and she punched in the number.

"Hey you," she said when he answered.

"Hey back, my lovely lady."

"I have two steaks."

"I have a bottle of wine."

"How long …"

"I'm downstairs. I was just waiting for you to call."

"The front door will be unlocked."

No need to let good money go to waste on that lovely number she bought at Victoria's Secret. She bound up the stairs by twos, freshened up, changed into the sexy red outfit, dabbed some cologne on her inner thighs and stood at the top of the stairs.

Jesse entered the front door and called her name.

"I'm up here, Jesse."

He looked up the stairs and nearly dropped the wine. Slowly, in heels that were way too high, she made each footfall closer to him count, her breasts bouncing freely in the lacy outfit. He was devouring her with his eyes as she allowed each long leg to extend before her foot touched the stair. When she reached the final step, she landed onto the hardwood floor with the clicking of her heels and sent blood rushing through his body. Jesse turned his back to her and double checked the door to make sure it was locked, grabbed his small bag, removed something from it, and turned back to face her as he sat the wine on the floor.

"Damn, damn, damn," was all he said as he snatched her into his arms, struggling to get his pants down, putting on the protection and kissing her all at the same time. "Help me, Savannah," he pleaded as he struggled with the zipper, still trying to land kisses upon her mouth. His boots were already by the door. He kicked off a pant leg to better position himself as he hefted Savannah up in his arms, impaling her with his desire. Calloused hands felt magical as palms, rough like a loofah, caressed the soft skin on her buttocks, lifting and lowering her rapidly as he thrust his hips upwards to meet the downward pulling of her body to his. She cried out as she found her release immediately, followed soon by Jesse's.

He clung to her tightly, almost afraid to let her go for fear the magical spell would be broken. It wasn't his best performance, but he was past gone. Even if he was only hers for just one night a week, he would take it, for now. If behind these closed doors they could create a world for just the two of them to be safe and enjoy one another, he would.

Savannah disengaged first, lowering her legs to the floor. "I assume you liked the lingerie?" she asked, looking down and realizing he had ripped the panties.

"Sorry, I will replace those. I just can't seem to get my fill of you. I just ... aahh damn." He kissed her once more and found himself needing her again. He grabbed her by the hand and pulled her up the stairs, kicking his pants off as they went. What Jesse truly needed was a bed to take care of round two.

Chapter Six

Forty-five minutes later, the two descended the stairs hand in hand, feeling pleased, satisfied, and very hungry. Jesse created a quick marinade for the steaks as Savannah placed the rolls on a pan to be placed in the oven. She washed the lettuce, tomatoes, carrots and cukes before carefully slicing the vegetables for the salad. Then she placed the grill pan upon the eyes of the stove to get hot for the steaks. She handed Jesse an apron since he stood at the stove adorned only in blue boxers, which he admitted he had recently purchased to turn her on.

As she sliced the tomatoes, she looked at the magnificence of his body and needed to know if she too, was sharing him with somebody else. "Jesse, do you belong to someone?"

The meat sizzled as it made contact with the grill pan. "I'd like to belong to you," he said under his breath.

"Is that so?"

"A man walks in the door after a hard day's work, you greet him in that red sexy number, then make dinner, cook him breakfast, and pack him a lunch for work the next day! Who wouldn't want to belong to a woman like that? What is it you want, need, or I can give, so that I can belong to you?"

Savannah laughed. "What I could use is a new car. Mine is 10 years old and has an attitude problem."

Jesse flipped the steaks. "How do you like your steak? And what kind of car do you want?"

"Medium well and a C-class would be incredibly nice."

"What color?"

"Sapphire Gray Metallic, four doors, for the kids and the dog of course." She smiled as she gazed up at the ceiling.

"How many?"

She looked at him as she went to the cabinet and handed him two plates. "How many what, cars?"

"No, kids. How many kids would you like to have?" he asked as he plated the perfectly cooked beef cuts.

"At least three. I think that's a good number. It is just my brother Jerwane and me and sometimes, I wish there was a third party you know, to referee. What about you?"

"There are three of us. I'm the oldest."

Savannah uncorked the wine and allowed it to breathe while she sat the salad bowls on the table. Jesse blessed the food and cut into the steak. It tasted like manna, considering how hungry he was. His appetite was only heightened by the two rounds of acrobatics in bed with such an amazing woman. If there was a means to discern what had gone awry in her relationship with her soon-to-be husband, it was none of his concern. It was well understood by him, his psyche, and his overzealous penis, she was not his to keep. Something in her relationship was broken and he was the temporary fix. If anyone thought long and hard enough, there was always an obvious answer to any problem. There was definitely a gap in her life that she was currently allowing him to fill. The man she was engaged to was very stupid to be missing out on what he was so happily enjoying. The selfish side of him wanted more than the two helpings he had been served. He wanted access to the whole pantry, but it wasn't his kitchen he was eating in. It wasn't his table he was eating at and he had not even paid for the food on which he feasted. However, in his defense, he had been invited inside to share the meal. No one could blame him if he gulped down everything presented to him.

He felt like he was addicted.

Jesse thought about the poor fellow in the parking garage that she had sprayed with cayenne pepper. *Had he been given a serving and was that the end result?* This was only his second dose, but after the first, he had his schedule rearranged to ensure that on Thursdays he was free by five o'clock and somewhere on this side of town, if not in this complex. There were so many burning questions, but this was only his second invitation. In the morning she could have a change of heart and end all of this just as quickly as it had begun. Maybe, if he understood the woman, he could understand what was driving her and why he was here. If it became clear to them both or voiced by either, that would be a place to start a conversation. In the interim, he planned to be back next week and the week after and the week after that. But first, he had to open a dialogue.

"Savannah. What do you do at the university?"

She explained that she was a doctor of letters and an instructor at the College of Sciences. "Really, I fancy myself as nothing more than a research technician with a small stream of alphabets behind my name. My research focuses on African Americans with high blood pressure as well as the metabolic disorders in the modulation of mitochondrial protein phosphorylation by soluble adenylyl

cyclase which ameliorates cytochrome oxidase defects."
Jesse's face went blank and his jaw dropped. *Who the hell
had that problem*? What the hell *was* that problem? *Did
she just curse me out in science*? His face was registering
all of his thoughts, which caused her to smile a bit.

"It sounds impressive, but honestly, that and two
bucks will get me a pack of hotdogs," she said and she
pierced a carrot.

"Are you one of the top people in your field?"

"Yes, but at the end of the month, after student loan
payments on the overpriced alphabet, this mortgage and
utilities, I barely have enough wiggle room left over to
feed myself, hence the 10-year-old car."

Jesse attempted to process the pieces of the puzzle
Savannah had carefully supplied, telling him something
he couldn't put his finger on, but yet, subtly understood.
He was eating her food. She had bought them steaks. This
was not purchased by her fiancé. "When is the wedding?"
he asked with more than just curiosity.

"Valentine's Day, next year," she said slowly as if she
were giving him a deadline to do something as she made
eye contact with him.

"So, either I have a year, or I have a year."
Savannah had no idea what that meant and allowed it to
roll off.

Jesse stayed the whole night with her again and held
her close after making love to her once more. In the
morning, she fed him a hearty bowl of oatmeal with
apples, brown sugar and raisins and handed him his
lunch as he made his way toward the door.

It would be seven more days before he would feel her

beautiful skin against his again. The way she responded to his touch, his directions, and how she freely gave of herself in bed started his blood to boiling. A week was too long. He pulled her in close and kissed her in a way that made them both want more. "Aahh damn," was all he said when seconds later, she found herself straddling him on the couch for one more round before he left. Jesse could not seem to get his fill of her.

*Addic*ted.

Next month, he would probably be the poor bastard in the parking garage, holding his nuts and crying after being sprayed in the eyes and mouth with cayenne pepper. In the interim, he was going to hold on to every moment with her. Somehow he managed to eventually get out of her apartment while she headed upstairs for a quick shower and found herself running late for work. In her haste, she nearly forgot her lunch. She opened the fridge to find an envelope, in the same colored stationary as his business card, braced against her pink DNA-stranded lunch bag. She opened the flap and pulled out $300 in cash along with a note scribbled in a bold male script:

"For the lingerie, dinner, breakfast, lunch
and some wiggle room for the month.
You have the number."
-Jesse

"Damn," she said aloud. She was in trouble, because she was really starting to like Jesse Orison.

Chapter Seven

March

It was a gorgeous Saturday afternoon. Savannah dressed in a new pink tea dress that she had purchased at Steinmart with some of the money Jesse had left for her. Three hundred dollars may not seem like a lot of money to many, but when you live paycheck to paycheck, $300 is a windfall. She and Darwin never discussed money and unless it was a large expenditure like her car's maintenance, he never offered her any. He paid for what he felt she needed and gave her jewelry and gifts on the appropriate occasions. He seldom concerned himself with her day-to-day living. Funny, she mentioned it once to Jesse, who eyed the empty plate and realized she spent extra to cook him a steak dinner and left her money. *Thoughtful.*

Savannah parked her Ford in guest parking at the Mountainbrook Country Club instead of using the valet service. One, she was embarrassed about her car, and two, she didn't really have enough cash to properly tip the valet. While she was in Steinmart, she had found a nice pair of matching sandals on sale for ten bucks and she thought she would get those as well. Her one designer bag was the basis for the dress of choice, and she entered the country club in a good mood.

The mood was soured by Darwin's mother, who first

complimented the dress, then systematically picked apart everything she wore, including her lack of nail polish. Darwin's sister came to her rescue saying, "Mother, really, must you be so harsh?"

Cassiopeia Finney Lockett was a moderately attractive woman who had married a white man of money and power, whom she never saw. He traveled extensively and refused to give her his seed to create children. Occasionally he would show up for dinner. It was well known through social circles that he married her as a tax shelter and to keep other women from trying to trap him into marriage. The only thing Henry Lockett liked more than fast black women was fast money. Savannah smiled at her for coming to her rescue against her mother, but inwardly, she cringed at the irony of the whole scenario.

Cassiopeia was a constellation and a Greek goddess, known for her unrivaled beauty. This woman was a small gas giant, with bad skin, flawed diction, and a fondness for flavored vodka. She often smelled like cotton candy and booze. She did love to shop and Savannah had been fortunate enough to be the recipient of Henry's platinum card. The soon to be sister-in-law had given her a pair of gold hoop earrings, price tags still on, and a pair of very high heeled designer shoes that were not fit to be worn in public. Jesse did appreciate those last month though. Cassiopeia also gave her an overcoat she so desperately needed.

A lack of the basic necessities can make a woman change how she feels about herself. Financial compromises to personal integrity can be replaced with a desire for personal gain. Savannah was tired of struggling financially. This said little for the conversation she was fraught to stay focused on. She drifted back into the conversation to find they were discussing white doves.

"I don't want doves, Mrs. Finney, they do tend to poop when they are flying and I would hate to have my guests hit with bird droppings," Savannah told her.

"Nonsense dear, the doves will be released out the side door of the church, it will be grand, trust me." Mrs. Finney patted her on the arm and continued the conversation about daylilies.

Savannah objected, "Daylilies are very pricey out of season and February is out of season." Once more she was overruled and she began to itch. The itching turned to stinging and stinging turned to burning. Her face felt like it was on fire.

Cassiopeia's eyes grew wide with concern, "Oh my God! Are you having an allergic reaction?"

Savannah's hands flew to her face, which was now very warm. She rummaged through her purse and found a compact and opened it. She jumped with a small scream as she peered into the mirror to find she had broken out in hives. Mrs. Finney wanted to ensure her son's soon-to-be wife did not make a spectacle of them all and encouraged her to use a side door.

"Please forgive me, but I must leave."

Neither of her future relatives rose to see her out or even bothered to see if she was okay. The valet walked her to her vehicle and she cranked up the car, overcome with the need to get away from those two women. She drove a short distance and began to hyperventilate. She pulled her car into a private drive and grabbed her phone.

She punched in the number and he answered on the second ring. Her breath was quick and shallow, the tears had started to flow and what came out of her mouth was pure gibberish.

"Savannah? Are you driving?" Jesse had just come down from the roof to meet with his cousin Bart about a project they were working on and asked his cousin to wait a moment.

She muttered, "No."

"Good, sweetheart, tell me what you see in front of you."

"I see a tree, Jesse. A pine tree."

"Good, my lovely, focus on the bark. Notice the detail of the bark and think of all the little lives that tree is supporting. Slow breaths, okay, you have to slow your breathing."

He stayed on the phone with her until her breathing had evened out. His face was laced with concern as he went to his truck to pull out his tablet to check his schedule. *What can I reschedule if need to get to her?*

"I'm sorry, I just had a panic attack or something, I am so sorry to have bothered you, I just dialed ... the phone." The tears were wiped away as her head leaned against the steering wheel.

"It's okay, but the question is, are you?"

"I'm good. Thank you, I really mean it."

The line got quiet as she broached the subject of Thursday. This week was not a good week, since her *Aunt Flo* was visiting and she suggested he should not come over. For a second, Jesse experienced a moment of panic. His heart rate increased and his eyes darted left and right, then he started to breathe hard. He wanted back into her home. Bart reached for him, but he held up a hand indicating he was okay. He wanted back into her arms and he was not going to allow her to get away so easily. Jesse wanted to belong to her.

In a hushed tone, he whispered into the phone. "There are other things we could do, you know. I enjoy being in your company, and this doesn't have to be about sex." He held the phone and waited. He was still uncertain of what *this* was; he just wasn't ready to let go of any of it yet.

"What are you suggesting we do to occupy ourselves?"

"Well," he said. "There is still that tube of Astroglide."

"I'm hanging up on you," she told him as she found herself smiling and enjoying his deep throaty laugh on the other end. Since being with him, she found herself smiling more often.

"Do you play chess, Savannah?"

Savannah was very pleased to know that he didn't mind spending some time with her outside of the bedroom. It emitted a warm and fuzzy feeling on her insides. This was only heightened when she confessed to being on her high school and college chess teams.

"Well, set up the board and be prepared to bring it, Science Girl," he told her with some intentional goading.

"You need to brace yourself, Tool Boy. You're going to get sacrificed." She paused for a minute, thinking about how calm she felt now in comparison to five minutes ago. "Which is your favor?"

Jesse was silent for a minute. "I am starting to enjoy the idea of having my own black queen." He got quiet when he heard her voice catch. "I will be a few minutes late, but I should be there by 6:15. If anything changes between now and then, you have the number."

He hung up again. Savannah wished he'd stop doing that and at least say goodbye first.

Sunday after church, Darwin inquired about her outburst at the country club. After politely explaining to him it was an outbreak and not an outburst, he still reprimanded her like a child. Instead of having dinner at her mother's, he decided he would treat them to dinner at an all you can eat buffet. "Your mother tends to really like these kinds of places," he told her as he ordered from the menu and they trudged to the bar.

He invited her back to his place, but when she informed him of her condition, he drove her home instead. She invited him in and asked if he would like some coffee and maybe play a game of chess with her. Darwin scowled at the sheer suggestion that he spend an evening playing board games.

It was unfair to make the comparison between the two men. In her book they were both using her. The saving grace was one she enjoyed and the other she had learned to stomach. If she were able to take the better traits from them both to make one man, her life would be grand.

Chapter Eight

It was a nice quiet week and it somewhat troubled Savannah that without Darwin at her heels, she was more relaxed. Because things had gone so well in the lab, she left early to head home. She made a quick stop at the grocery store, and picked up a whole chicken and a bottle of white wine. As soon as she arrived home, the bird was quickly washed, seasoned, stuffed, and placed in the oven at precisely 4:30. She tidied her kitchen and dining area, and set up the chess board. An idea popped into her head and she quickly ran up the stairs to check the guest bathroom. Got it!

The condo was simply decorated in a French Country theme. It was the simplest and most efficient means to make old furniture look antique and charming. The few pieces she had, she painted or used sprays to patina pots. One wall in the living room was accented with a French Country blue paint and adorned with a canvas that she had smeared color on so it looked abstract.

The Essex couch, the focal point of the room, was a hand me down from her boss, who, after two children, realized a white couch was not doable. The coffee table she made from the do it yourself section at Lowe's. It was finished off with some decorative trim and careful staining. The matching end tables she also made herself. The dining room set she had found on Craigslist from a woman who was leaving her husband and needed a quick sale. With the help of her brother, Jerwane and his truck, she picked up the pieces for $250.00. The spare bedroom was her old furniture from her mom's house and her bedroom set was the first new pieces of furniture she had purchased. The mattress was not low end, but it wasn't the highest end either. It slept well and she was happy with her place. Everything in it was paid for and belonged to her. The condo and her education were her only debts. It was a nice feeling.

A nicer feeling came over her when the doorbell rang at six twenty and she opened the door to find Jesse standing there with a huge bouquet of flowers. "These are lovely. Thank you." She let him in and took the arrangement.

"It smells heavenly in here. Is there anything I can do to help?" he asked as he kicked off his boots and grabbed his small bag. "Savannah, is that apple pie I smell?"

She grinned with pride as she stood at the sink arranging the flowers in the one vase she owned. It too was bought off Craigslist from a woman who was not aware it was Wedgwood crystal. It was one of the few items she had of value.

"Yes, it is. We also have ice cream, which I plan to gently dust with a bit of cinnamon." She turned to find him standing in the kitchen entry staring at her as if he was trying hard to balance out his breathing. She gave him a warm smile. *Damn he is sexy.*

"Hurry up and wash the day off you. The chicken is almost done, as well as that yummy pie!" But he had not moved. He eyed the dining room table with the chess board set up, the table settings, and her with the vase of flowers. *Home. It felt like home.* Jesse was uncertain of what he had done right to walk into this woman's life, but he was here and loving every minute of it. Whoever her fiancé was, fancy diamond ring or not, he was about to uproot his garden. *I want to come home to this every day. I want to come home to her.*

Jesse showered quickly and changed into some clean clothing. When she told him that the evening would not be as usual, he headed by a big box store on lunch break to pick up something casual to wear. As he came down the stairs, Savannah was pouring the wine and making his plate. He could not help himself. He pulled her into his arms and kissed her. "Thank you, for all of this. It looks wonderful."

She patted him on the chest and urged him to sit. He blessed the food and cut into the chicken. His eyes rolled up in his head when he tasted the perfectly seasoned meat. The apple pie garnered the same reaction when he bit into the slice of heaven. She poured them each a cup of decaf coffee and Jesse leaned back in the chair, full as a tick, patting his belly.

"How were things this week at the lab with your research on mitochondrial oxidase effects on high blood pressure?" He grinned at her with a set of pearly whites that seemed to lighten his face when he asked the question.

Savannah's eyes grew wide, impressed that he had remembered, maybe not all of it, but enough to let her know he had heard what she said. "Do you remember the rest of it?" She asked curiously.

"Of course," he said as he sipped his coffee. "It was the effects of high blood pressure on African Americans followed by some big fancy science word, and blah, blah, blah, blah, and blah blah." He started to laugh, along with Savannah. *Funny.*

She told him about her week then asked about his. Jesse was very careful in his word choice, which prompted her next question to him, "Are you single?"

"The only woman I am currently seeing or being intimate with is you." The words hung in the air like a sour ball of gas, but Savannah would not walk into the stink. Jesse took the cue and rose to clear the table while watching Savannah portion out the leftover chicken. Thin slices were cut from the breast meat and placed into a container. The dark meat portions were thrown into a food processor, leaving the wings and broth as a base for soup. Jesse had never seen anyone so efficient.

"I let nothing go to waste," she stated matter-of-factly. Savannah left that hanging in the air along with his statement. "Let's play some chess."

By 9 pm, her brain was cramped. They played three games. Jesse won two. He asked again about the guy in the parking garage. She explained once more that they never dated and only had a few classes together in college, but there was never anything between them.

"Is your fiancé also a black man?"

Savannah was shocked by the forthrightness of his question. "Yes, he is." Quickly changing the subject to her surprise of the evening, she put on the kettle and brought out her Dr. Scholl's foot bath. Jesse eyed the contraption as if it were a medieval torture device. "Just what exactly are you planning to do with that?" he asked, suddenly feeling extremely uncomfortable.

"I am planning to use this on your feet." A simple explanation was given as she removed his socks and rolled up the legs of his lounge pants before placing each calloused foot into the soak. She poured cold water from the sink into the soaker followed by hot water from the kettle. Similar to the way Vietnamese women performed the ritual in the pedicure shops, she scaled off the years of rough skin that had formed on his feet from wearing closed in shoes all year. Then she used her electric file to smooth down the big toe nails that had gotten hard and clumped from rubbing against the steel in the toe of his boots. Savannah massaged his soles and applied a tingling mint foot cream before she bagged up the newspapers containing the clippings and dead skin. Finally, she dumped the foot soak water down the toilet.

"Feels pretty good, doesn't it," she asked when she returned to find him rubbing his feet.

She expected a nice thank you and maybe some making out but instead, again, he hit her with a weird direct question. "Do you do this for him, too?"

"No, he has it done at his male grooming salon." She twiddled her thumbs then looked at the clock.

Jesse stood slowly, extending his arms to reach out to her. "This past month with you has been a truly eye-opening experience for me. I have never felt so cared for and I'm not sure what to say or how to handle all of this Savannah."

In truth, she had no idea what she was doing either. Jesse was only the fourth man in her entire romantic life. Never had she experienced such intense chemistry with another human, nor had she ever been so sexually free.

Their lovemaking was noisy.

It was sloppy.

It was unordered.

It was fantastic.

Even tonight, as they were unable to couple, he held

her close in the dark with his need poking her in the back.

If felt like a slice of chocolate cake on the day she started her diet. She could look at it, but not enjoy it, not in the way she wanted to. "Do I need to help you with that?"

It took him a moment to understand her question. "No. I seem to always be in this state when I am around you. It'll go down." Hell, lately even if he wasn't around her, he was still in this state. Jesse chuckled as he went into a bit more about his week.

"Last weekend I was fishing with my dad," he started as the darkened room filled with the sound of even breathing and his voice. His hand rested loosely on her hip, his leg intertwined with hers, holding her body close to him.

"I cast my line into the river, almost entranced by the bobbin floating on the water, just thinking I know how that bobbin feels, drifting on the currents." He kissed her shoulder as he pulled her closer to him, the back of her thighs resting against his. "I started thinking about how good it felt dangling my pole over the water, then I thought about another spot where I love to dangle my pole...." His words wandered off into the darkness of the room.

"Then, I got a bite. I jumped up so excited, trying to reel in my catch and completely unaware of my state...." He paused for a minute. "My dad, who missed his calling as a comedian, told me, *Son, why are you so excited, it ain't even that big of a catch!*" He could feel the shudders of Savannah's body as she laughed quietly in the dark.

Jesse kissed her shoulder as his hand ran down her hip, settling on her thigh and eventually ending on her lower abdomen. "I ignored him, because he has no real idea how lucky I am to have made this catch."

Goose pimples formed on her arms at his words, her response given in a lowered tone. "We are both lucky."

Jesse surprised Savannah the next morning by making her breakfast and serving it to her in bed. While he showered, she packed their lunches and ironed her clothing for work. She kissed him goodbye, bidding him a good day as he stood in the doorway looking back at her, his face adorned with his usual Friday morning quizzical gaze.

Savannah asked, "Is everything okay, Jesse?"

"Yes, it is. Thank you for a wonderful evening. You have the number." Then he was gone.

During the course of the day as he traveled from site to site checking on construction projects, he found his stomach grumbling. Several of the workers had taken a break for lunch on the side of the new building and Jesse joined them with his brown bag. This was something new for him since he rarely, if ever, brought a lunch, but it was also an ideal time to connect with his new crew.

Several years ago he had been engaged to an enchanting woman with really large breasts and a moderate ability to reason. The relationship failed because he couldn't talk to her. They had very little in common even though she was from a construction family. As much as he tried to explain what it was he did for a living, the hours he worked, and the irregularity of his schedule, she had never once packed him a lunch. Fast forward to his current status. His schedule was far more flexible, his pay so much better, and he could have whatever he wanted for lunch, any day of the week. He was excited to join the crew and open his lunch sack, just to see what Savannah had packed for him to eat today.

The guys watched him as well as he removed two roasted chicken breast sandwiches on whole wheat, a bag of mini carrots with a small container of ranch dressing for dipping, along with a zip lock bag of white seedless grapes and another zippy bag with whole almonds. *Healthy.* In his world, little containers and zipped plastic bags meant you belonged to someone—a someone who took care to ensure you ate right.

He looked into the bag again and he literarily poked out his lip. There was no apple pie! His phone chimed as he looked down and saw the message.

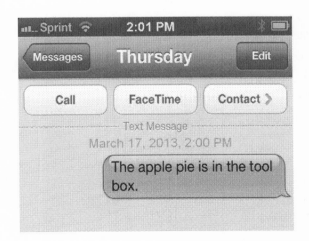

What a woman! Whoever the stupid bastard was that had allowed him to creep into his flower bed was in for a world of trouble. Jesse was considering becoming that troublesome weed that would take root and infest everything. He was in. It was going to be difficult to get him out.

Chapter Nine

April

Savannah was freaking out a bit about the engagement party on the fifteenth. There was so much to do. Her arms needed more toning, five pounds had to be dropped, a new hairstyle was a must, and, of course, make up. The latter was something she seldom wore or had little use for, but understood it was required for a polished look.

On a Monday evening after Zumba class, she sat in the Smoothie King on 28th with her friends Sheryl and Traci. They were lying to each other about their weight loss plans. If intention could move the world forward, she would be a size six instead of a ten, but she was healthy. Savannah was five feet seven and 130 pounds with a natural hairstyle. She was grateful that her grandmother was a Choctaw Indian, which gave her long thick locks of shiny black hair. The texture of her hair and features had been passed down from her Grammy. Unfortunately, a low tolerance for alcohol was included in that genetic pool, but overall she considered herself to be somewhat attractive. Unlike many of her friends, she was not one of those women who harped on her looks.

Men often stared at her, but that meant very little to a woman of science. Science nerds flirted often by waving or wagging their big dictionaries to impress the academic side of the big brain she carried, but the woman in her was coming to life. Of the four men who had passed through what she attempted to call a romantic life, Jesse was the only one who sparked the sexual side of her. In the garage on that first night, the attraction between the two of them was undeniable. Helping with his bleeding nose and seeing all of those muscles uncovered made her want him with a fierceness she had never known. It was never her style to be wanton, but each time he entered her, she climaxed. Whether it was a short interaction or something more time consuming, she came like one of Pavlov's dogs at the ring of a bell. It was wrong. She knew it was wrong, but after she got married, good sex would be out the window. The getting was good and she was going to get all she could.

Her phone chimed and she looked down to see the caller I.D. read, *"Tool Boy."* She answered on the third ring. "This is Savannah."

Jesse's smooth timbered voice resonated through the phone. "I want to see you."

"We have an appointment on Thursday, if I am not mistaken," she said into the phone as Traci and Sheryl took note of the conversation.

"What if I don't want to wait that long?" he asked.

"Thursday at six is the scheduled appointment. If something changes and you can't make it at that time, please let me know." She was smiling when she added the last bit, "You have the number." Savannah hung up on him. Damn, that felt good. She felt powerful and was smiling like a fool.

Traci, who was always rather inquisitive, scratch that, she was plain nosey, asked, "Who was that, the hairstylist?"

Savannah was never one to tell lies. Yes, she could live

one, but not tell one. So she decided to be honest. "That was my maintenance man."

Both friends nodded as if they understood. Savannah was hit with an idea. She sent him a text.

On Tuesday she joined Darwin and his coworkers for drinks after hours at a bar on Highland Avenue. She wore a fitted black dress, a splash of color around her neck that matched her shoes, and carried a clutch bag. Her hair was up, with loose tendrils framing her face. She even had on a dab of lip gloss. As an extra measure, she added some mascara to her already long lashes, which made her feel pretty. Everyone at the bar agreed. Darwin looked at her with new eyes.

"Savannah, you are absolutely glowing. You look amazing," he told her as he showed her an unusual amount of public affection. She worked the room, mingled with the other wives, and passed out compliments as well as thanked those who lavished compliments upon her. It was a pleasant evening.

Darwin seemed anxious to get her back to his place. Still seated in her newfound power, she played with it a bit. "Quite honestly dear, I truly hate your bed. We will need to go mattress shopping to get something we both can agree upon." She kissed him passionately, left him in need, and climbed into her car headed home.

On Wednesday, she was headed to the mall, but decided instead to venture into a Lingerie Shoppe on Montevallo Avenue, which was nice for her wardrobe for Darwin, but not quite what she needed for tomorrow night. A sly smile crept its way across her face as the naughty side of her began to imagine his reaction to an outfit she had always wanted, but had never been daring enough to purchase. *Daring is my middle name.* What she needed for her next encounter with Jesse was something nasty.

She knew where to go.

Chapter Ten

Savannah set the table for dinner, checked on the pork chops and headed for the shower. At six on the dot, she heard the front door open and heard the clank of the toolbox hitting the floor. Her body reacted to knowing he was inside the condo and soon he was going to be inside of her. Her mouth wasn't the only thing salivating.

She approached him with slow deliberate steps as she planted her feet with a wide stance and gave him a full view of her new outfit. As he unlaced his boots, looking up at her slowly, noticing immediately the patch of hair that extended from the lack of a crotch in the lacy lavender silk panties. Jesse closed his eyes as he inhaled the intoxicating nectar of her readiness for him. His eyes slowly wandered up her torso to the laced sides of the bra that appeared to be missing the cups. Savannah's erect nipples protruded from the fabric. Jesse's rough, calloused hands traveled up her thighs until he stood upright, facing her with his senses on overload and his need to be with her straining against the fabric of his pants.

"Damn," he said as he reached for her. Savannah jumped back, almost recoiling from his touch, which shocked him.

"Every time you say that, I end up either supine or in an impaled positioned becoming enervated after being contorted into some form of a coital pretzel."

Jesse's hands went to his hips. Each word she said caused his head to cock a bit more to the right, finally ending at a 45-degree angle. He appeared to be listening carefully while seeking understanding of the explanation of the Affordable Care Act. He repeated her words out loud, "supine ... enervate ... coital pretzel ..." followed by a gigantic smile on his sexy lips.

Savannah's hands flew to her hips as well. "It means ..." Jesse cut her off.

"I know what the words mean. I went to college, twice, and graduated both times. You have some vocabulary on you there, my lovely." He continued to talk as he loosened his belt and removed his pants, placing them on top of his toolbox. His arousal was evident and Savannah was fidgeting in her eagerness to have him inside of her.

"I'm sorry, I meant no offense," she said as she reached for him, but he held up his hands, indicating he needed to wash the dirt from them before he touched her again.

"None taken," he told her. "Keep in mind that I work with men whose vernacular is laced with innuendos and limited to finding new synonyms for the word vagina."

"Will you share the funniest one you ever heard?"

His laughter rang out from the bathroom, "Soft shelled tuna taco." He burst into laughter, which echoed through the apartment.

Savannah started to laugh as he took care of his quick cleanup, returning to remove a condom from his overnight bag.

"My senses are on overload right now. You, using big words, stimulating my brain," he told her as he gently tore open the condom wrapper. "Dinner smells absolutely delicious, stimulating my belly and reminding me of how hungry I am." He held the condom in one hand while pulling down his underwear to free his erection with the other.

"Then there is you, lighting up every sense in me. I can smell you. Your scent is filling my nostrils, exciting my brain, and letting me know that you are ready for some coital pretzeling."

Savannah smiled at him as she held the sheathed readiness in her hands. "So what would you like to eat first?" she asked with a wicked smile. The answer was already known as she turned and walked toward the stairs, her ass firm and moving like cat stalking an unsuspecting prey. Jesse followed behind her with his wand pointed at her as if to cast a fairytale spell.

Jesse climbed the stairs behind her. "That is a dumb ass question." The stairwell was as far as they got as Savannah's forearms rested on two stairs ahead of her and her knees rested two stairs below. Jesse was behind with his face planted deep within her vertical smile. It was almost embarrassing for Savannah. Her mind had been anticipating his arrival all day, causing her to be so worked up that all it took was a few strokes of his tongue and she was starting her ascent. By the time Jesse took the nub of flesh into his mouth and suckled, she was calling his name.

"Not yet, Baby, not yet," he pleaded with her.

"It feels so damned good and I have been waiting for you all day," she whispered into the wood of the stairs. "Now Jesse, now, please right now."

It was a good thing that Jesse had braced his hand against the banister. As he inserted the beginning of his intention, Savannah thrust her hips backward, sucking him into the vortex of her love. The force of her orgasm pulled him along for the ride as he pumped furiously, emptying two weeks of backed up fantasies about being with this woman.

"Savannah," he whispered her name, resting his head on her shoulders. The words he wanted to say were stuck in his throat. Whoever *he* was would have this. *He* would come home to those beautiful dinners, have a packed lunch every day, and get to wake up next to this woman.

He hated that idea.

He hated feeling like he was on borrowed time. He hated sharing her.

But, she was not his.

He had nine months to make a change in the landscape. The next step was to plant some kudzu. If he was going to take care of the weeding, he may as well take over maintaining the whole damned yard.

In the darkness of the bedroom, the glow from the alarm clock revealed the time. It was five thirty and the alarm would ring in another half hour. It was too bad Jesse's body was already awake, craving Savannah's attention. He wasn't a pig and he wouldn't fondle her in her sleep to wake her so that she could take care of what he needed. She would be awake soon. He could wait.

The clock now read 5:37. Only seven minutes had passed and he was having a mental conversation with the blue veined throbber that was screaming for release. *I can't believe how hard my junk is right now.* His only thought was her.

He needed to be inside of that body; that sweet, luscious, giving body that loved the feel of him when he entered her private palace. The feel of her surrounding him, warm, delicate, and hungry made him grow even harder. How her body gripped him so tightly each time he entered her and she responded to him, coming undone in his arms. A man could get used to that. The feel of her breasts against the hairs on his chest, her firm thighs locked around his hips, thrusting upward. The sound in the back of her throat as her orgasm built and those eyes....

Jesse liked to make love to her with the lights on so he could gaze into those deep brown pools. He loved watching her pupils dilate when he would give her long strokes during her orgasm, driving her crazy.

5:45.

He would not make it another 15 minutes. He was so hungry for her, he wanted to roll her onto her back and mount her like a prized stallion, rutting until the hardness eased off. His fingers ran across her abdomen. He wanted to slide his hand lower into that sweet valley of delight and get his fingers wet. *She tasted so fucking good, like ambrosia with extra cream.*

"Savannah," he whispered in her ear. "I need you."

Her long legs rubbed against his as she stirred in the darkness. 5:47.

It had only been 10 minutes.

"Savannah baby, wake up," he said again as he reached for the nightstand to grab some protection. She stirred again, pushing her ass against his erection. *Fuck, I'm not going to make it if she does that again.*

Jesse reached for the nightlight and clicked it on. Savannah moaned as she stretched out on her back.

Jesse was sweating. "Baby, please wake up. I can't hold on much longer, please, wake up."

Savannah turned to face him, eyes heavy with sleep. "Jesse, what's wrong?" He grabbed her hand and slipped it under the covers.

"My junk is harder than Fox News on the President. I need you so bad, please wake up and help me."

Her hand held him and stroked him a few times. Jesse didn't want her hand. Anxious fingers tugged at her panties, pulling them down her thighs, over her knees, across her ankles and tossing them on the floor. He slipped between her thighs and buried his face, licking, lapping, and moistening.

Savannah moved against his mouth, moaning and gyrating her hips. "Yes, Jesse. Yes, that feels so good."

Enough. He had enough. Like an animal, he crawled up the bed, lifted her hips from the mattress, aiming, throbbing, and needing her. He pressed forward as he thrust into her. "Aarrrrhhhh," he growled as he thrust even harder.

He whispered into her ear, "I can't get enough of you Savannah." He kissed her neck. "No matter how much you give, it never seems to be enough." He thrust harder, feeling her tighten around him. "So good, Savannah, this is so damn good."

She clawed at his back as he unleashed his desire upon her, squeezing her thighs, pulling at her hips to meet his thrusts. She cried out his name.

The alarm clock sounded as Jesse reached his climax, grunting out her name. His breathing was ragged and labored as he lay atop her, holding on to her body, still inside of her, not wanting to come out.

Addicted to something that is not mine to keep.

Jesse Orison grimaced at the anguish of what he was experiencing. He wanted her for his own.

Chapter Eleven

Savannah chose to wear a simple lemon chiffon dress with a high satin pink waist to the engagement party. Judging by the reaction of Darwin's family, you would have thought she had walked in wearing a thong and a smile. It was April. Spring had arrived, it was an attractive dress and it made Savannah feel pretty, which showed as her skin glowed and her eyes shimmered. Many of the men in the room shared the sentiment and Darwin was displeased that she had drawn so much attention to herself. Mrs. Finney made a snarky comment that Savannah did not appreciate. It left a sour taste in her mouth, which she soon found a reason to regurgitate.

"My dear, you look like lemon frosting on a baby shower cake. Whatever made you think that dress, in that color, was a good idea?" Mrs. Finney asked Savannah while she looked down her beakish nose.

Savannah's time with Jesse and the freedom to express herself in the bedroom was spilling over into her everyday life. She was no longer afraid of Mrs. Finney. Each day, she was becoming less afraid to live from paycheck to paycheck. It had served her well for the past five years. Hell, one or two more would be worth it versus having to deal with that insipid woman. Her mother had taught her when she was asked a question that she should be polite and give her answer.

"It is no worse of a concept than having a bunch of doves shitting all over my wedding guests. Yet, you seemed to think that having them is a good idea, so we

72

are even. Now, if you'll excuse me," she said as she walked off to talk to Cassiopeia. Maybe she misunderstood the polite part. Savannah fully comprehended that if she didn't gain some control over Mrs. Finney, there would be no means of reeling that woman in once the children were born.

Savannah went back to enjoying the party.

The guests were all lovely. The few friends that Savannah and Darwin had in common were there to wish them well, but Savannah would rather be home playing chess with the handyman. She had left her car at Darwin's, leaving the ride back to his place filled with thick tension in the air. Mrs. Finney had complained about her mouth and the dress. Darwin was torn. He wanted to make love to her, but she only wanted the evening to be over. This was not fair to either of them. *What are you doing, Savannah?*

Had Darwin done anything to earn this treatment? All of this was her fault and her doing, coupled with a dose of bad judgment. Jesse should not be in her life and he damned well didn't belong in her bed. She had to break it off before it became more serious. Yet, she felt like a fanatic when it came to Jesse. The smell of him. The feel of him inside of her. His ability to make her come undone each time he entered her.

It was the choice she had made. Darwin was going to be her husband. However, as she lay under him, listening to his misguided attempts at pleasuring her, the timing of the whole scenario was incredulous. The night she got engaged to Darwin was the same night that Jesse showed up to rescue her from a failed attempt by a man who wanted her as a notch in his belt. *Was that what was*

73

happening between her and Darwin as well? Was Jesse rescuing her from a failed attempt at having a happy life?

Imagining a lifetime of lying under Darwin and pretending to enjoy his lovemaking took some work. This man barely knew where the little man in the boat lived, whereas Jesse could drive up, sending him paddling and sending her through multiple levels of orgasms.

Darwin was just going to have to be taught how to please her body.

A weird feeling came over Jesse as he sat at the table listening to his mother prattle on about wanting to remodel the kitchen. It had been remodeled three times in his 34 years of life and he asked his parents if they had thought about living somewhere smaller. His mother reacted as if she had been scalded and his father gave him a stern, disapproving look. Nothing was tamping down the unsettled feeling roaming through his belly giving him gas. Something was off.

He jumped up from the table, startling both of his parents and scaring the wits out of his 4-year-old cousin. It was his cousin Bart's son, whom his mother Ruth brought over to rub in her children's faces and remind them of how it felt to be grandchild-less.

Jesse grabbed his phone and checked it for messages. The feeling would not go away. Something urged him to call or text, but he opted instead for a cool glass of water and some deep breathing. Savannah was planning to dump him. He just knew it.

"Son, are you okay? You act like you saw a ghost or

something," his father said with a look of concern on his face.

"I'm all right Dad. I just need to think some things through." He took his glass of water and headed out to the patio. This was his childhood home. He grew up here and loved coming over for dinner once a week. His parents were getting older and were dealing with many changes in their lives. Jesse was also struggling to come to terms with some of the changes in his.

Since meeting Savannah, Jesse's train of thought about where his life was going had switched tracks. As the eldest son, he was being groomed to take over the family business. It never entered his mind to do anything other than work construction. When he was five years old, he had learned to wield a hammer. Like his father and his father before him, they were construction workers. They were men who used their hands for a living. A piece of wood in his hands could be molded into anything from a piece of furniture to a toy.

When had things moved to the point of me becoming some woman's plaything?

Sadness filled him as the epiphany flashed across his face. He had been happier in the past three months with her than he had been in the past five years. Behind her closed door, they were both free to relax and enjoy each other. If he was able to change her mindset of his role in her world, he could increase the possibility of becoming something more to her. Thoughts soared through his head as he mentally cataloged each room of her condo. There had to be something that could connect them together. He set his glass on the small patio table he had constructed in a high school shop class. The tables! The tables would be the connection.

Jesse walked back in the house with a smile on his face. He had a plan to become more than just her maintenance man. There were other things in her life that he could also tighten up and repair. However, the first thing he had to fix was his role in her life.

Chapter Twelve

May

Savannah watched Jesse as he eyed one of the end tables she had made. One of the screws had not seated properly, which made the second table a bit wobbly. He went to his tool box, grabbed a few items and corrected the screws. The old holes were sealed with wood putty leaving the table to stand strong.

"Thank you," she said coyly. "I made those tables."

Jesse nodded. "I was wondering, Savannah, since I am here once a week, is there a bigger project you would like to start that maybe I could lend you a hand with?" It was the perfect bait and switch. He showed her the creeping ivy, and he just needed her to think it was a good idea to plant it.

Her eyes were wide. "You would be willing to do something like that with me?"

"Sure," he said as he sipped on the perfectly brewed and sweetened decaf iced tea. "I mean, we need to work on something to justify me coming over here every week with a tool box."

Savannah was thinking she liked playing with his tools, but it would be cool to build that headboard for the guest room. "I really wanted to build a headboard for the guest bed." She told him how she truly wanted to build a frame for the bed with at least six storage drawers underneath to maximize the space.

Jesse asked for a piece of paper. Together, they drew up a sketch of what she wanted. He knew that one night a week was not going to get it built in a timely manner. He would need to come over on Saturdays as well. Savannah was skeptical, but he would need some time to get the plans made. In return he asked for a favor.

"Can you make meatloaf?" he asked.

Savannah thought it was a weird question. "Yes, I can."

Jesse's face went all soft as he told her how every other Tuesday his mother would make meatloaf. On Wednesday his dad would have a meatloaf sandwich for his lunch. "I would love a meatloaf sandwich in my lunch bag, as well as some sour cream mashed potatoes with gravy and green beans for dinner."

His eyes were sparkling. Savannah found herself wanting to please him. "I could do that next week for you. I leave for New York on Monday, but I'll be back on Thursday morning."

Jesse rose to find his pants. He located his wallet and pulled out a $100 bill and gave it to her. "This should cover anything you need to buy."

"Jesse, it does not cost a hundred dollars to make meatloaf and mashed potatoes."

He perked up. "Ooooh, add some crusty rolls and some grape Kool-Aid to the list."

Grape Kool-Aid? Did this gigantic grown man just ask me to make some grape Kool-Aid?

"Jesse, what you have requested will not take all of this." She looked down at the bill. He opened his wallet and pulled out a fifty and handed that to her and she handed back the hundred.

"No keep them both, use it to stock up the pantry or buy something special you like to eat."

He was so different. Jesse found ways to give her money without her ever having to ask. Darwin, on the other hand, would take her to get what she needed. *Stop it.* These men were very different. Comparing the two was unfair.

"Savannah, I am looking forward to building something with you," he told her as he watched her face reason through whatever was filling her head.

"Building something with me?" she repeated, uncertain of what he meant.

"I would like it to be a life, but I will take what I can get. If we start with a bed, we are at least starting."

"I like that bed idea." She smiled at him. "I like your tool too." She was being brazen, but she didn't care. Her body loved this man's touch and shamefully, so did she.

"Tonight, Savannah, I want to show you how I make love." He pulled her close and lifted her into his arms. He was slow moving up the stairs as he whispered loving words into her ear. Call it what you will, Savannah just wanted him. So much for her plans to end it.

On a Monday afternoon, Savannah boarded a plane to JFK for a quick shopping trip in New York for her wedding dress. The excitement of visiting the Big Apple waned when she arrived at the airport to see Cassiopeia in line beside her soon to be mother-in-law. Her mother, Emurial, had ridden with her and held her tongue when she saw Darwin's mother. It was with a smile that she hugged her soon to be in-laws as they chatted briefly about their plans when they arrived in New York.

What plans? Who needed a plan? All Savannah wanted to do was see an off Broadway show, have dinner at B. Smith's, and hit Kleinfeld's for a dress. Darwin had provided her with a prepaid credit card with a limit of $1,500. She had to shop smart. The money she had saved for the dress, added to what he gave her, limited her options.

Although she had not asked, Jesse slipped a few bills in her wallet along with a note that said, *"Just in case."* This was the money she was going to use to take her mother to see a show with and then treat her to dinner. All of the plans her in-laws tried, had gone awry.

Savannah knew exactly which dress she wanted. It had always been her fantasy to wear a cream-colored sheathed lace gown with an illusion neckline and capped sleeves. She knew the designer and the budget, but she just didn't know how difficult Mrs. Finney could be. After trying on fifteen dresses, Savannah's nerves were worn thin. Her mother, on the other hand, was showing amazing restraint and patience. The final gown was the one that Savannah loved. It was in her price range, required no alterations, and could be shipped to her home for no cost.

Mrs. Finney hated it. Cassiopeia told Savannah it made her look fat, which caused Emurial to tear up and walk away for a bit of fresh air. That was enough. Savannah turned to Mrs. Finney and said, "This is the dress I want and the dress I am going to buy."

"Dear, you can't be serious. That dress is dreadful, and is unflattering to your figure," she said as she eyed the dresses on the rack.

Savannah didn't know where it came from or what made her say it, but the words rolled out her mouth. "Not that it really matters, but your son has no idea what to do with my figure or anything else with my body."

Mrs. Finney's breath caught. Cassiopeia opened her mouth to spout something venomous, but Savannah held up her hand. "And unless you are planning to pay for this dress or anything else, your two cents is also unneeded. Quite honestly, you could have kept your ass at home. This was a time for me and my mother. I allowed you to tag along as a courtesy to my fiancé, but upsetting my mother is not acceptable."

Emurial had just walked back in on the tail end of what Savannah had said. Her eyes were wide as Mrs. Finney got indignant. "Savannah sweetie, why are you being rude? You should watch your tone. They were only trying to be helpful."

Savannah twirled in the mirror to take another look at the dress. "Helpful to whom, Mother ... Satan? I have simply reached my limit of being treated like a child. It is *my* wedding, it is *my* dress and I," she turned in the gown, "Am going to wear what *I* think makes me look beautiful."

Her mother smiled at her with new respect when she asked, "So, Mother, what do you think?"

"I think you look stunning, sweetheart," she said as she touched the delicate lace across the shoulders.

Savannah told the shop girl that she would take the dress. It was on sale for $900, which left her with more than enough to do some other things for the wedding. The shop attendant inquired about veils and Savannah admitted she would make her own, as she paid for the dress.

Mrs. Finney was furious. "When my son hears about this...." was all she was able to muster, when Savannah turned and handed her the iPhone.

"Call him." She hit the speed dial and the phone began to ring. "He will care as much about this incident as he does about what I am making on Tuesday for dinner." When Mrs. Finney refused the phone, Savannah took it instead, using the speaker function.

"Hello, Darling," Darwin said into the phone. "Have you found the perfect dress?"

"I have my love, it is so beautiful. It is too bad you are going to have to wait until February to see me in it." She paused for a moment and then continued, "I have to warn you though, your Mother and sister hate it." She eyed the two ladies who were now sulking.

His laughter rang through the shop. "Those two hate everything, unless they personally hand pick an item."

Savannah laughed along with him. "I came in well under budget too. I can use the rest for some other items for the wedding."

"That's my girl," Darwin said as he told her he loved her before hanging up. Savannah turned to her future mother-in-law and said, "My mother and I plan on seeing an off Broadway show, then we're going to grab some dinner at B. Smith's. You are more than welcome to join us or feel free to do your own thing."

They opted to do their own thing, which pleased Savannah to no end. Emurial looked at her daughter. "What has gotten into you? I love this newfound confidence."

Savannah loved it too. It felt good to speak her mind. She wanted to be honest and tell her just exactly what was getting into her every Thursday night, but that would just be tacky. She opted instead for a moment of honesty.

"Mother, I am 29 years old. I have spent the past twelve years staring down at a text book or a test tube." She applied some lip gloss, and then let down her hair.

"I am not about to let two women who have lived empty lives dictate to me how I am going to live mine." Her mother's eyes widened as Savannah shook out her hair. "I am brilliant. I am sexy. You can bounce quarters off this ass and my beautiful breasts are real." She winked at her mom and said, "Thank you for these and really good genes," as she jiggled her C-cups. "I feel alive!" She looped her arm through her mother's and headed out the door. She pointed at the soon to be in-laws who were climbing into a cab. "That is not my life and it will never be."

Emurial hugged her daughter. When she learned of the engagement, she prayed a silent prayer asking God to watch over her daughter, who was marrying well, but marrying safe. There were many benefits to living safely, but happiness was seldom included in the package.

Savannah opened her arms wide, staring up at the skyscrapers and twirling in the middle of the crowded sidewalk. "Let's go spend some money, Mother." Emurial watched her daughter saunter down the street with a sway in her hips and a sashay in her step.

This was not good.

Emurial recognized the signs, but kept quiet. The only question that popped into her head was why Savannah had spent a thousand dollars on a dress that would never make it down the aisle.

Chapter Thirteen

Savannah arrived home on Thursday morning, excited for the remainder of her day. She unpacked, washed, and put away the items from New York, which included a tee shirt for Jesse and a collector's pin for the new cap she had purchased for him. She placed those items in the downstairs closet.

She had also purchased a coffee mug for Darwin's desk and a snow globe that would be perfect for his home office. Around 2:30 she headed toward the grocer's to purchase items for the meatloaf dinner. She started making dinner at 4:30, taking extra care with the mashed potatoes. The doorbell rang at 5:45, surprising Savannah. Jesse was early. She opened the door and found Darwin standing there.

"What a surprise!" she exclaimed as she let him inside. She had to get to her phone to send Jesse a text. Darwin held her in his arms and kissed her with a newfound passion. He smiled as she kissed him back. "I guess you must have missed me."

Darwin was extremely affectionate tonight. He asked a million questions about the trip and the dress, and chatted about how angry his mother was, especially the part about him not knowing her body. The air became impenetrable with unsaid words that could change their future. "Darwin, I was just ..." He rose so suddenly that Savannah felt threatened.

"Savannah, I know I am not the best lover, but I am willing to learn how to please you and be better."

Savannah was at a loss for words. The tension that filled her only worsened when she heard the knock at the door. Thank heavens she had locked it when she let Darwin in. It was normally left unlocked for Jesse.

Oh crap, the potatoes were boiling over. As she ran to the stove to turn down the eye, she looked back, realizing that Darwin had gone to answer the door. She heard Jesse's voice and the two men were talking. She didn't know what to do, so she started making the mashed potatoes. Jesse would leave, she would send Darwin home, and have Toolboy come back later. Simple enough.

It wasn't.

Savannah turned to see her fiancé and her lover both standing in her kitchen, staring at her.

"Darling," Darwin asked. "Were you expecting the maintenance man?"

Jesse held up a tube when he made eye contact with her. "Yes. Jesse, are those the plans for the captain's bed?" She was impressed with how calmly she stated the words.

"Yes, Dr. Niden. I have the plans and two separate budgets for the bed. If it is not a good time, I can come back another day." He used her formal name and title. Damn, that turned her on. Maybe next time she would wear her lab coat and have him call her doctor as he spanked her ass with those rough, calloused hands. *Focus, Savannah*. She had not heard the familiar clank of the toolbox by the door and felt a minute of relief. It was brief.

Darwin interjected. "We are about to have dinner. Would you like to join us? I also would like to hear more about this bed project."

Both Savannah and Darwin looked at Jesse. Savannah

smiled and waited for Jesse's refusal but instead Jesse opened the container with the plans. "I would love to stay. Dinner smells delicious. Is that meatloaf?"

Darwin frowned. "Meatloaf?"

Jesse eyed him curiously, asking if he disapproved. Darwin, rolling in his pretentiousness, said the meal was so common, further insulting them both by adding that his fiancé enjoyed comfort foods. "That of course will have to cease once we are married and she starts to bear our children."

Jesse's eyes never left Savannah, who inhaled deeply. "Can I help you with dinner Dr. Niden? Maybe set the table or something?" Jesse asked.

"No, I have it." She went back to work making the mashed potatoes. Darwin began to bombard Jesse with questions about how he and Savannah knew each other and how this bed project came about. Jesse sat at the counter in the kitchen and stated that he had met her at Lowe's in the millworks department.

The next two hours proved very interesting for Savannah. Not only did she learn a great deal about Jesse—and Darwin—she learned a great deal about what she valued in a man. Darwin was suspicious by nature and relied heavily upon status. His opinion of Jesse changed when he found that Jesse was an engineer who also held an MBA from the University of Alabama. Jesse's family were legacy builders with the Crimson Tide. He explained that both of his parents were graduates as well as his grandfather, his grandfather's father, and his grandfather's grandfather.

Halfway through dinner, Darwin noticed Jesse's polo shirt and began to blitz him with questions about

Montgomery Construction. Jesse said he had worked for the company off and on during the summers in both high school and college and now served as a project manager for Savannah's building complex and one other in Bessemer. Darwin was condescending when he told Savannah that Montgomery had built the complex in which she resided, with each unit custom tailored to the condo owner. He added another insult to her by blurting out that her unit was one of the low-end models with few frills.

"I am not sure if you are going to be able to sell this at decent price. If you do find a buyer, you really can't count on much of a profit." Savannah continued eating, trying desperately to make the meatloaf go down her throat.

Darwin only pushed the food around on his plate and declined to drink the Kool-Aid. Jesse complimented the food, telling her she was a great cook and thanking her for sharing their meal with him. Darwin went on and on about Montgomery Construction. He hinted that his company was bidding on the new project coming up in Riverchase. The ground had been broken, but the firm and project manager for the designs had yet to be selected.

"I would love to be the project manager for that site. It would mean a lot of long and late hours, Savannah, but it would be a feather in my cap and could put us on easy street."

Jesse began to ask Darwin questions, starting with his name. The fiancé joked about his sister's name as well, confiding their mother was a former English teacher who prided herself on being a learned woman. Next, Jesse asked about other projects Darwin had designed. Last, he asked about his familiarity with the condo models that Montgomery constructed.

Darwin piped up like a little chick, telling Savannah, "Of course, since each condo is custom, the architect is needed on site to make modifications to each unit."

Savannah watched Jesse as he assessed Darwin. She watched Darwin assess Jesse. This was surreal. The two men in her life were literally as different as night and day. A fleeting thought crossed her mind that if she could just combine the two, she would have the perfect partner.

Jesse helped clear the table as Darwin sat and watched the interaction between the two of them. Both men declined dessert, which led them right into the plans for the captain's bed. Darwin was unclear on why it needed to be constructed since she would be moving in with him in a few months. Jesse's jaw clenched and his face twitched. It was so brief that if had she not been looking at him, she would have missed it. He didn't utter a word as he walked her through the plans for the bed, explaining that cost would shift based on the type of wood and finish she wanted.

"Why don't I just take you shopping and buy you a bed for the guest room Savannah?" Darwin asked with some frustration when he looked at the complexity of the project. It also troubled him that Jesse would be here with his woman helping to build it.

She had said very little the whole evening. She looked at her fiancé. "I want to learn how to do this Darwin. I take pride in things that I create and I want to make this. It means a great deal to me."

Darwin slipped his arms around her waist and kissed her temple. "If it means that much to you, then of course,

Darling, whatever you want."

Jesse had seen enough. "It's getting late; I have an early morning. Again, thank you for dinner." He extended his hand to Darwin and told him it was a pleasure meeting him. Jesse just wanted to get out of the small space that seemed to be consuming all of his oxygen.

"Wait, Jesse," Savannah said as she went to the kitchen and sliced several pieces of meatloaf and put them into a reusable container. "I cooked way too much and as you can see, Darwin is not a fan of my meatloaf."

With a quick nod of his head, he replied, "If you have any problems with the plans just let me know, but you should be able to do most of it by yourself."

Darwin breathed a sigh of relief as Jesse gave a nod and was gone. It would be futile to tell her not to be around the man, since Darwin knew that doing so would only make her gravitate towards him. "He's a nice guy," Darwin added. "How long have you been seeing him?"

Savannah's eyebrows went up. "What do you mean?"

Darwin smiled a sheepish grin. "I mean, my Darling, you obviously have spent some time together formulating this idea. I asked how long you two have been hanging out."

"It has only been a few weeks. We met and discussed the project. I ran into him in the parking lot, then again at Lowe's where I told him my about my idea. We created a sketch last week and here we are." Savannah kissed Darwin on the forehead and inquired if he was planning to stay the night.

He did not.

He left soon after. Jesse did not come back either.

Chapter Fourteen

June

Two weeks passed and she had not seen or heard from Jesse. Darwin had gone with her to Lowe's to buy the supplies, helping her select quality pieces of wood. He helped with the selection of hardware and discussed finishing options with her. He even purchased her a sander, a power drill, and girly tool belt. Darwin made two more surprise visits, seeming stunned to not find Jesse at her home helping with the construction of the bed.

She missed him. She wanted to see him and needed to be with him. The phone seemed to magically appear in her hand. Damned traitor! He answered on the third ring, "Hello."

"I miss you," she whispered.

"Really?"

"I want to see you."

The line was quiet. She fidgeted, but continued, "What have you been doing?"

"Working on a few things." Jesse said no more.

Savannah understood. "Okay. I was just checking on you. I'll let you get back to work."

The line was quiet and she heard him exhale, "Savannah?"

"Yes, Jesse?"

"I miss the hell out of you too," he told her.

"Tomorrow is Thursday."

"I will be there at 6," he said and then hung up.

Darwin called on Thursday morning. He was excited. He told Savannah he had a meeting that evening with the team from Montgomery Construction. A wayward strand that filtered from a random thought danced across her mind as she wondered if Jesse had anything to do with this meeting. She dismissed it as silly, and coincidental, and she prepared for her evening.

"She lit candles in the living room, put a light scent on her thighs, and dabbed a bit of the perfume between her breasts." Jesse arrived at 6:00. He was wearing black slacks with a shirt and tie and dress shoes. He looked so handsome.

He skipped dinner and made love to her then quickly got dressed to leave. A shiver ran through Savannah as she lay in bed trying to sort out the feelings threatening to overrun her. A futile attempt at gaining control over her emotions and getting a better grip on the sensations coursing through her mind failed. The frustration of being so close to understanding what she was feeling really got to her. The tears started to flow. She touched her cheeks and was surprised by the outpouring of liquid from her eyes. *Where had that come from? Why am I always crying around this man?*

Jesse sat on the side of the bed and gathered her in his arms. "Don't cry, Science Girl," he told her as he gently rocked her. "Savannah, I don't know what you want from me. Am I your diversion until your marriage or do I mean something to you? If you just wanted sex then I gave that to you, but this is getting complicated."

Her body shuddered with tears as Jesse held her close. "My Lovely, I don't know what to do. I am not that kind of man, but you make me feel and want things that I don't have any right or claim to. I want to come home to you and lie down next to you each night then wake up next to you every morning. You are not mine and I believe I am hoping for something that will probably never happen. I can't do this, it has to stop."

She wiped her eyes and stared up at him. "Do what your heart tells you to do, Jesse."

"But I don't want my heart broken." He kissed her lightly. "This is scaring me and if I get out now, I think that I can save myself."

Savannah wasn't ready to let him leave her life, her bed, or her heart. It was selfish and she knew it, but Jesse was her private oasis. He quenched a thirst in her that she did not know she had and right now she needed more. She needed him.

"It's too late," she told him as she unbuttoned his shirt and loosened his belt buckle. "If we are to drown, then we do it together." She kissed him with a ferocity that ignited his passion. "If you give to me, I will give back."

"You promise?" he asked with some uncertainty as he began to give in to her touch. *Addicted.*

She reached inside his pants and grabbed him and began to massage the stiffness of his hesitation. She nibbled at his neck and earlobes and tugged at his hair. "If you take care of me, I will take care of you." Savannah pushed him back on the bed and grabbed the protection from the nightstand, applying it to his readiness. She climbed on top of him and lowered her body over his need.

"You promise?" Jesse's eyes closed as he phrased the question, trying to maintain some form of control. "You are going to be my Kryptonite, aren't you?" he asked as his hands reached for her.

"Jesse," she whispered his name and began to slowly move her hips up and down. "If you love me, I will love you back."

He quickly worked his way out of his pants and rolled her to her back, looking down at her with loving eyes. "You promise?"

"I promise," she whispered to him, as he slowly made love to her, connecting them on a new level. It was a bad idea and he knew it. She knew it, but they were getting in deeper. At the end of the journey, someone was going to get hurt. There was no way around it.

The room was softly lit as the two snuggled under the covers, each one mindful of questions, concerns, and the fear of losing what they had found in each other.

"Savannah," he called her name softly as she snuggled closer to him, her body indicating she had heard him call her name. "Why me? I mean, have you dated a white guy before or am I one of those things on your bucket list?"

Savannah slightly raised her left leg, allowing her calf to drape over his as she rubbed her soft leg against his very hairy one. "I have never dated a white guy before. You would be my first." She continued to rub his leg with hers. "I guess," she paused to collect her thoughts. "The night in my bathroom, when I touched you, everything in me came to life. Since then, I have never been more alive, filled with this new energy. I think if I try, I can do anything or be anything. I feel ..." she paused, "... whole again, when I'm with you."

Jesse kissed her shoulder, tugging at a lock of her hair.

"What about you, Jesse? Do you have a love of darker berries?"

He was quiet for a moment. "No. You, too, are my first."

"Why me? If I may borrow your question."

Again he was quiet. "Great peace."

Savannah bolted upright in the bed. "Do you mean p-e-a-c-e or p-i-e-c-e?"

Jesse pulled her back down into the bed, flinging his thigh across her legs as if to hold her steady. "P-e-a-c-e," he spelled back to her. "I think I was five years old when I wielded my first hammer."

In the past few months, Savannah had learned that he needed a few minutes to gather his thoughts with a usually spot-on analogy. She listened intently when he explained that he was a certified brick mason, as was his father, his father's father, and his father before him. "I am also a certified welder, a certified electrician, and a certified H.V.A.C. mechanic. No one can walk onto my job site and tell me something about a project without me fully understanding what they are talking about. But ..." he paused briefly. "... there was never a question of what I would be or do when I grew up."

Jesse explained that he came from a family of construction workers. The women he had dated all came from construction families. "If I had continued on that path, I would have married one to unite the family businesses. As the eldest child, it is given that I will take over after my father retires."

Savannah said nothing as she waited for him to bring the words back full circle. "The night you kissed me in your bathroom, I went home a bit uncomfortable, but I slept."

She turned in the bed to face him, wanting to understand.

"I have not slept well in seven years." He kissed her on the nose. "That is, until I met you. I go home at night and sleep so comfortably, restful and content."

His eyelids drooped a bit as if he were giving up the battle for sleep. He muttered the next words before drifting off, "I am cared for, loved, and I finally belong to someone. I am at peace."

Soft snores filled the room as she lay there in the soft light of the lamp watching this gigantic man, covered in muscles, callouses, and way too much body hair. He was a gentle giant who wanted nothing more than to be loved and cared for. It seemed simple enough because Savannah knew she had started to feel deeply for him as well.

Chapter Fifteen

Saturday at 11 am, Jesse arrived with his toolbox and Chinese takeout. He didn't want her to cook on a Saturday. Outside on the small covered patio was the completed headboard that Savannah had meticulously worked on. Jesse checked the joints and corners, and eyed the small finishing nails she used to connect the pieces. He was impressed with her use of the sander to smooth out the edges on the wood.

"I thought about covering the headboard with padding and fabric, but I love natural wood best," she told him as she walked through the steps she had taken to complete the headboard, including the whitewood ornaments used to enhance the clean lines.

"This looks really good. One thing though," he told her and she waited for his criticism. "The back has to be stained as well to protect the wood even though it will be against the wall." Savannah stood there blinking at him, still waiting for him to tell her it was not good enough, but he didn't. Instead, he took a look at the plans and noticed she had modified the drawings. He went to work on laying out the frame for the bed.

In less than an hour, the structure of the first side of the bed was complete. They took a quick break for lunch. As they sat at the kitchen counter she explained some of the changes she had made. The original drawing was too bulky and she liked the open squares better, for books, baskets, and options. Jesse ate in silence. A bit of sawdust and shellac was in the tresses of her hair. He stood close as he removed the bits of flakes until they were all gone, finally running his fingers through her hair.

"Savannah, can I ask you something?" He said as he held the jet black strands in his fingers. She flinched a little, uncertain of what was coming, but told him to fire away.

"I noticed several black women patting themselves on the head. What is that about?"

Savannah stopped chewing and looked at him with uncertainty of where the question came from. But now? It was weird. "They do it because their scalp is dry and itching."

"Why not just scratch the itch?"

"It will loosen the bond or the stitching of their hair extensions," she said and went back to eating her chicken and mixed vegetables. Jesse stared at her in utter confusion. Savannah explained that oftentimes hair extensions are either sewn or glued in. After several weeks of sweating and no air to the scalp, it begins to itch. "Scratching can loosen the bonds or stitches as well as flake up the dry scalp, so the women pat themselves on the head instead to keep the style intact." Jesse glanced at her hair.

"This is all mine," she told him with a chuckle. He inquired about the thickness and length. "My grandmother was a Choctaw Indian. My mother has many of the Indian features. I inherited the nose, hair, and some of the coppery undertones in my skin. My brother, Jerwane, looks like a black American Indian."

He stared at her face, taking it all in. The next question nearly made her fall off the stool. "What kind of hair would our children have?"

Instead of panicking, Savannah allowed the scientist in her to take over. She talked about recessive genes and dominant traits, including the fact that since they were both dark haired, the child would most likely have dark hair. "However, there is a high probability of the child having a dusky blonde colored hair, simply because of the mixed races."

Jesse went back to his lunch then back to work, only stopping once that afternoon to ask, "When is your birthday?"

"November 8th," she told him as she hammered the nails into the wood, double-checking her work with the level, ensuring the sides had been put together evenly. "When is yours?"

He held the other side of the wood, joining his piece to hers as she drove in a nail. "August 24th."

They stopped at the same time and looked at each other. Jesse added, "That is supposed to be the ideal match, cosmically."

"I was thinking the same thing," she said before she shrugged and went back to work on the bed.

By the end of the evening, both sides of the bed were complete. The only things left to do was build the base, stain it, and move it to the room. She was pleased with what they had accomplished. Jesse patted her on the back and packed his things.

"You're leaving?"

"Yes, let's not push our luck." He stepped inside and closed the patio door. In the kitchen, away from prying eyes, he took her in is arms and kissed her. "I will see you on Thursday evening."

Chapter Sixteen

July

Jesse sat in the conference room at Montgomery Construction staring out the window. Although he was not alone, his thoughts drifted into nothingness as he questioned the morality of the choice he was about to make. In his heart, he was not this type of man.

The bids for the contracts for the Riverchase units were up in the air, and he held the deciding votes. It would be easy to award the contract to a company that had worked on other projects, but it might be wise to allow another firm the opportunity to be a part of the Montgomery Construction team. The plans were simple. The ground had been broken and the utility lines were being put into place. In a month, the concrete would be poured and the architect would begin meeting with the new condo owners. There was little room for error, and at this late stage, it would be foolproof.

If the contract was awarded to Green & Associates, the firm which employed one Darwin Finney, then that man would be occupied for at least six months to a year. New homeowners were fussy. They were picky and they took a great deal of finesse and handling. Jesse wasn't sure that Darwin possessed the capability to do the job, but his credentials were impeccable. This type of project would either make him a better man or show his true colors. One thing Jesse was certain of was something he had learned first-hand—these types of projects took a toll on relationships. In order to do it right, the hours required would wreak havoc on a fledgling marriage. Assigning this project to Darwin Finney would end his relationship with Savannah.

He heard his named called, but refused to answer as he pondered a choice that would say a great deal about the type of man he was becoming. Jesse held up his hand begging for a moment of private thought. Sweet thoughts wandered to Savannah's beautiful lips, those long silken cinnamon legs, and a sweet spot that tasted like nectar from the gods. His body was reacting to the thought of those legs wrapped around his waist. When they were in bed, she gave herself freely, holding nothing back and satisfying him in a way that resonated into his soul.

Jesse's brow furrowed when he again thought of Darwin coming home to *his* dinners, *his* meatloaf and mashed potatoes, and *his* homemade apple pie and grape Kool-Aid. His breathing became ragged as he imagined her packing Mr. Insensitive's lunch for work. He could *almost* stomach the idea of sharing her love with him, but it was the thought of her belly being swollen with that asshole's child that pushed him toward the edge.

He didn't want to be this type of man, but she was making him fight for her love, her affection, and his Thursdays in Savannah. *Fuck it.* He hated sharing and Darwin had to go. Jesse popped to his feet, alarming everyone at the table.

"I say we assign the contract to fresh eyes. Let's go with Green & Associates, let that Finney guy serve as the architect. He can't screw it up any worse than Jacob did on the last one." He left his notes on the desk and made his way for the door. It was Thursday and there was a beautiful woman awaiting his arrival. Both the dinner and the loving would be hot and ready when he walked in the door.

On Sunday, he would head to the church and pray for his sins, but right now there was one sin that was calling his name. His smile was genuine as he pulled from his assigned parking space at Montgomery Construction and hit the road. He punched in her number. She answered the phone with an actual purr.

"I am on my way to stroke that kitty."

Darwin sat at the dinner table on Sunday with Savannah and her mother with a gloat on his face. He was totally pleased with himself, as he bragged to both of them about being named as the lead architect on a new job. This was awful. Savannah found herself excited for him, but not for the same reason.

He leaned back in his chair and sipped his coffee, boasting about the number of hours that were required to do the job well. Savannah's only thought was the number of hours she would be free to be with Jesse. His birthday was coming up and she wanted to do something special. The chances of doing something outside of her condo were small, but behind those doors, she could do whatever the hell she wanted.

She and Jesse had laid out a few smaller projects after they finished the bed to ensure his Saturday visits, but she wasn't sure what she was doing. Her patience with Darwin had increased as he tried to learn how to please her body, but it always ended the same way. Six minutes of heavy breathing, four short thrusts and he would be done. Some attempts had been made with penile rings to lengthen his staying power, but sex for Darwin was about him. His feelings, emotions, and sex drive were all compelled by his selfish need to please himself first. A life of sexual frustration seemed less appealing each time she lay under him and lied.

Chapter Seventeen

August

Jesse wanted to be honest with Savannah, but their entire relationship was built on an untruth. Tonight, there was no sex. Jesse had something on his chest and it was not moving. This had a direct effect on what was not happening in his pants. He took a deep breath as he gazed deep into her eyes. "Savannah, I am in trouble here."

Her hands rested upon his, with eyes encouraging him to say what was troubling his heart. It felt like a blow to the chest when Jesse admitted, "I am falling hard for you." He spoke softly. "I had a say in the awarding of the contract." He waited for her admonishment.

"I understand what you are going through. It's a rough road we are traveling. I feel like warm, runny defecation in white pants," she said as she held his hands.

Jesse's eyebrows went up as he tried to imagine, but not imagine the image she had just given him. He shook his head, trying to remove the visual from his mind. Savannah rubbed the fine hairs on the back of his hands. "I know, but I'm happy to have him out of our way for a while."

There was no way to hide his frustration as he raised his voice to her, "Then why in the hell are you still planning to marry him?"

Carefully, using her words in a softened tone, Savannah explained that passion was great for keeping things interesting, but not required to maintain a long-term relationship. Nights of hot sweaty sex don't pay the bills, feed the children, or afford nice vacations. "I want a nice life, with nice things."

"But don't you want those things with a man who listens and appreciates you Savannah?"

"I have those things. What he appreciates in me is not the same thing you value in me. One can stand the long haul. The other goes away when my belly is swollen and I have no desire for sex."

Jesse was angered that she could only see him in a sexual way, regardless of the hours he had put into her projects to show another side of himself. "What about love, Savannah?"

The calmness of the delivery of her words was far more unsettling than her views on committing her heart to another. Love, she told him, was the one word the Bible took pages to define what it was not.

"Love ..." she told him. "... emptied my bank accounts and ran off to be a casino dealer in Biloxi. Without that money, I sat in the dark for two weeks, living by batteries and candlelight. I ate cheap salty noodles or leftovers from my mother's house for nearly three months. I went on dates with people I didn't like just to get a decent meal. I have not been upright since. I still live paycheck to paycheck, always afraid that something will get skewed and I lose everything ... again."

Jesse watched with some concern as Savannah stared him in the face, delivering a statement that nearly crippled him, "Love has never done shit for me but break my heart. I don't need love to survive, Jesse. I need security."

This was something they would disagree on and it was

hurting him. He had made a decision to reward a man with a job so he could have free reign with his woman. A woman who has just confessed she did not need, or believe in, love. Jesse's stomach rolled as he realized the complexity of his dilemma. He loved a woman who was not sure she knew how to love him back, although she promised she would. She lied to him, to get him into bed.

What was he thinking? She promised to marry the other sap and look at what she was doing to him. He thought about the guy in the parking garage who was obsessed with her. He had gotten a face full of pepper spray and a nut shot. He needed to get out of here and he needed to leave now. Once she touched him again, his power to do so left, along with his resolve. He had fallen into a trap, a trap he didn't think he could get out of, but there had to be a way to show her that she did love him and it was okay to do so.

Lake Purdy was beautiful this time of year. Jesse sat with his father, dangling a pole at the edge of the water, waiting for a bite. Big Sam, as friends and family called him, watched his son with some interest. Seeing there was something troubling his eldest child, he wanted, like any father, to fix the issue. He could see, however, that whatever was sitting on his shoulders was a big load.

Jesse was a great deal like his mother, Big Sam thought as he watched the snake make his way across the grass. It was nonpoisonous, so he said nothing as the reptile sought a place to shelter itself from the early morning sun. Big Sam adored his wife, but sometimes that woman made a mountain out of an ant farm and would overanalyze everything to the point of obsolescence. When it was all said and done, the simplest solution was evaded, only to be replaced by a long-term plan that was just too tiring to even consider.

"Son, whatever it is, it can't be that bad," Big Sam continued as he asked, "What is her name?" He cast his line into the water once more, keeping an eye on the little snake moving closer to Jesse.

"What makes you think I'm having woman troubles, Dad? I may just be having a rough time on the job." Jesse frowned, resenting his father's interruption of his thought process.

Big Sam whistled a bit and thought, *The hell with it.* "I know it's woman troubles because if it wasn't, you would have seen that snake trying to crawl up your pants leg." It was worth it just to see his six foot tall, two hundred and fifteen pound son screaming like a ten-year-old cheerleader while trying to shake the snake out of his pants. The shaking obviously wasn't doing it for Jesse, who decided to remove the pants altogether. He was still screaming and was now flapping his arms. He was whirling his pants about over his head like a fan flag at a Friday night football game. *Always with the overreaction.* It was still unclear why Jesse had removed his shirt, but Big Sam sat there chuckling as his half naked son's head snapped from side to side as if he was being flanked by an enemy horde of garden snakes.

"Sit down, boy, before you kill your fool self," Big Sam told him followed by, "The snake slithered off five minutes ago. Now put your clothes back on before someone calls the police on you!"

Jesse dressed in a hurry as Big Sam fired questions at him, starting with her name.

"Her name is Savannah." Jesse admitted as well as how much he was missing her after choosing to stay away from her the past two weeks.

Big Sam eyed his son's face as he asked the next question. "Her name sounds colorful and exotic. Am I understanding that correctly?"

It was now Jesse's turn to eye his father's expression. "Yes, Dad, she is part black and part Choctaw Indian." Before Big Sam could utter a word, Jesse went all soft and he began to extol her virtues. He told his father how accomplished and smart she was, that she was pretty, a great cook, and made fantastic meatloaf. "Dad, when I stay over on Thursday nights, she always packs me a lunch for work the next day." Jesse's eyes were still dancing as he told his father about the time she gave him a pedicure and sloughed the rough skin off his feet.

Big Sam asked, "What made her do that?"

Jesse's face was flat as he told his father, "She said my feet looked like I had been walking with Jesus."

A hearty gut-busting laugh poured from Big Sam. What made it even funnier was thinking about the first time his wife gave him a pedicure because of his rough feet. Big Sam wanted to know more.

Jesse hung his head in shame when he admitted that she was not his. He told his father how they had met, the immediate attraction, the mind blowing.... "Ahem ... sorry, Dad," ... the furniture building and chess playing. Big Sam asked how long they had been seeing each other and Jesse admitted it had been seven months. The father watched his son's head drop lower as he also admitted that the fiancé was a bit of an ass.

"How do you know that, son?"

"I had dinner with them one night," Jesse told him.

Big Sam laid down his pole. "Son, are you involved in some freaky sex shit with these two?"

Jesse explained that it was *his* meatloaf dinner she had cooked that night and that man got in his way. It was then that he admitted to awarding Darwin's company the contract, just to remove him from the scene. "Dad, I feel like I compromised my ethics just to have this woman."

"Son, the world revolves around the principle of the 3 P's: power, profit and poonanny. Wars have been started for a lot less. I am not sure how beautiful Helen of Troy was, but her face launched a thousand ships." He stood up and put his arm around his son's shoulders. "Your mother was dating a jerk. I intentionally ran him off the road during a drag race. His car caught on fire and I drove that rascal to the hospital, all the while comforting your mama, telling her he would be okay."

Jesse looked at his father with new eyes. "Jesse, eventually he was okay. But while he lay in the hospital, I took your mama to the prom, out dancing and romancing, and then I wooed her over to me. I have never looked back."

He turned Jesse to face him, his hands still resting upon Jesse's shoulders. "You are asking yourself the wrong questions, my boy."

Jesse's head popped up. "Son, there are two things you need to find out. One, how long have they been engaged? Second, why can you only come over on Thursday nights? Unless she is married, she is fair game."

"But Dad, she's promised to another," he said, still feeling a bit defeated.

"Son," Big Sam said as he went back to his pole. "People break promises all the time. She opened the door to let you in and has been allowing you to come back for 7 months. You owe it to both of you to find out why."

"I don't know Dad, I still feel it is dishonest," Jesse told him.

"If your intentions are just for fun and not for anything long term or permanent, then you are correct: your actions are dishonest. If you think that woman should spend the rest of her life with you, making your ma and me some cream-colored grandbabies, then stake your claim and make her yours."

"Daddy, are you okay with cream-colored grandbabies?" Jesse asked.

Big Sam never looked back at him. "I love you, Son. I will learn to love whoever you marry. My grandbabies could be purple and funny looking, but they would be mine and I am going to love them too."

Jesse threw his arms around his father, gave him a big wet kiss, and started to pack up their stuff.

"Hold on, Son, I'm fishing here," Big Sam told him.

"Not anymore, Daddy, I got work to do. Helen of Troy is awaiting me," Jesse told him as he ushered his father to the truck.

Big Sam mumbled all the way home, complaining that he failed to understand why Helen had to ruin his fishing. He was insistent, even when Jesse dropped him off at home, that he should conquer Troy on his own time, not when it was their fishing time together.

Chapter Eighteen

It had been nearly a month since Savannah had heard from Jesse. Her heart was heavy, but she knew it was for the best. Family and friends had begun to notice her withdrawal, as well as the noticeable demise in her newfound spunk. It was Tuesday. She sat on the couch with Darwin at one end and she at the other. He was doing some work on his laptop and she was pretending to read *Deep Fried Trouble,* the latest book by Tyora Moody. Her mind began to wander to the thought that if she were to die, would Jesse come to her funeral and reveal himself as her lover?

She smiled a wide grin, toying with the idea that she had a lover. *Had,* as in past tense. What had she done that was so terrible? She had been honest with the man she was cheating with. Life required order. Her life had to contain order. Monday and Wednesday were Zumba and paper grading nights. Tuesday nights she spent with Darwin. Friday nights she spent with the girls and Saturday, if it wasn't date night with Darwin, then it was her own as well as Sundays. For seven, glorious, sweat soaked months, Thursdays had belonged to Jesse.

When she looked up from her book, she noticed Darwin's mouth moving. "How goes your furniture building, Darling?"

She provided an artless answer as she spoke of a small unit she was constructing for the hallway to hold towels and necessities for the downstairs bath, freeing up some space for the small water closet.

"How is Jesse?" Darwin asked her with feigned curiosity.

There was no need for Savannah to lie so she told him the truth. "I haven't seen or heard from Jesse in a month."

Darwin closed his computer and leaned forward, resting his forearms on his thighs. "I thought for a minute, there was something more between you two. I was even more suspicious after I met him and was called in a week later to be interviewed for the Riverchase project."

Savannah said nothing as she watched Darwin work through his thoughts. "I hate to admit it, but when I got the assignment I thought he pushed me through to get me out of his way," Darwin confessed and watched her face closely. She gave away very little as she frowned, appearing to look confused.

"Get you out of his way for what reason, Darwin?" Her voice was sincere when she posed the question.

"To have unlimited access to you," Darwin told her, no shame in his statement.

Savannah was about to rise and move closer to him when her phone buzzed. It was 9:30 at night so something must be wrong. She asked Darwin to hold his thought as she crossed the room to get her bag. It was a message from Jesse.

She responded with a simple, *no*.

As she returned the phone to her bag, it buzzed again.

She responded again, *no*. Who did he think he was, giving her ultimatums and making demands on her time when he had disappeared for a month?

The next message confused, excited, and angered her all in one.

She cleared the message, placed the phone in the bag and sat back down, this time closer to Darwin, as he asked if everything was okay. She placed her hand on his thigh, rubbing it gently saying, "You worry too much about small things. It's unhealthy." She kissed him and initiated an episode of mediocre sex. Although she had made several attempts, Darwin just was not improving in his efforts to please her in bed. The truth, as she had been taught in church, will set you free. She said the words aloud as she stared at herself in the bathroom mirror.

My fiancé is a lousy lay.

Chapter Nineteen

Friday arrived and Savannah opted for a loose fitting black skirt, a lavender silk top, and a pair of comfortable shoes. She wore the skirt, along with crotchless undies, in case Jesse needed quick access.. Her need for him was bad. Her body was juiced up so she changed her underwear. It would be embarrassing to leave wet spots of her nectar wherever she sat.

He arrived at six on the dot, dressed in khakis and a red button down shirt. He looked as sexy as ever. She invited him in but he refused and escorted her downstairs to his truck. The crimson colored Ford F-150 had been washed, detailed, and shined up for the evening. The snarky side of her wanted to ask if he had his own car or if he just liked driving the company vehicle.

"I missed you, Jesse," she said as she slid into the passenger seat, making sure she allowed her breast to graze his arm.

"I missed you as well, Savannah," he added as he closed the door and walked around the vehicle. It was going to be a tough night, but Jesse had a plan. He was going to stick to it. Now, if he could just keep his boner from banging up against the steering wheel, he could get through this night. One touch was all it took from her and his body went ape shit. The skirt was making it worse. *Focus, Jesse, focus.*

"What is that scent you are wearing?" he asked after placing the vehicle in gear and maneuvering the truck into traffic.

"It's called Night Stalker," she told him, taking a small bottle out of her bag that was labeled the Pilgrim Soap Company.

Savannah smelled good enough to lick, eat, and swallow whole. She lifted the hem of her skirt and the scent of her ambrosia sweet nectar wafted up to his nose. Her body was ready and calling to him like a siren luring sailors to their deaths. *I don't believe it, my shit just got harder. Focus, Jesse, focus.* "I like it. I smelled it on you before. It's sultry."

They arrived at the Olive Garden and were seated right away. Jesse had been craving chicken marsala and liked the way they prepared it. Savannah opted for the appetizer of calamari and suggested they share. The dinner ticket with drinks only came to $31 and some change and Jesse was pleased. That was the cheapest he had ever bought dinner out for two people, especially on a date.

"I learned that trick several years ago. Order an appetizer and a meal, then split the food. It cuts down on the cost of eating out," she said with a smile.

Jesse was now getting a real understanding of how she had lived her life, skimping and cutting as many corners as she could to save a dime. The thoughtfulness was appreciated and her considerateness didn't end there. At the movie theater, she showed her faculty pass, which reduced the cost of her movie admission, saving him more money. Jesse had allocated enough money for the date and had only spent fifty dollars.

Inside the theater, they sat on the very back row. Savannah rarely went to the movies; it was not in her budget. Movies were limited to rentals from Redbox, but this was nice. When the lights went down, she placed her hand on Jesse's thigh. He took her hand in his and interlaced her fingers within his own. Savannah was not going to be discouraged so she uncrossed her legs, spreading them slightly and placed their joined hands in her lap. Jesse moved their hands back to the center divider between the seats.

This was insane. *He brought her to a movie to actually watch it! What in the hell was this movie anyway? Riddick.* Since she was not going to get a happy ending, she hoped the movie had one. It was an engaging film, but not a first choice for her. After the movie, he took her for coffee and dessert. Jesse opened the discussion.

An hour later, they were still bantering back and forth on the similarities between *Pitch Black* and the reboot of the new version. They argued about character flaws, script inadequacies, and the death of the dog creature. Even in the vehicle on the way back to her place, Savannah still felt the plot was predictable and she felt cheated not seeing the love scene between Riddick and Dahl. Jesse knew she was about to feel cheated twice.

He walked her to the door. "I enjoyed our date, Savannah. Have a good night."

Wait a cotton-picking minute! Did he think he was going to leave after he had stimulated her mind and body and reenergized her spirit? And now he wasn't even going to give her a mustache ride? Oh hell no!

"Jesse, aren't you coming inside?" she asked with some elevated degree of concern.

"No," he said as he headed for the stairwell. "Goodnight, my Lovely."

She took off running after him. "What is this? Is it

some kind of game?"

Jesse seemed surprised by the question as well as the next one, "Jesse, are you playing with my emotions?"

His face was solemn when he answered, "Are you playing with mine? You said if I loved you, you would love me back. Then you told me you didn't believe in love. You lied. I can't trust you."

Savannah pointed at the door, telling him this was not the place to have this discussion. He reluctantly walked inside and stood at the door listening, but not listening, to her diatribe about love, relationships, and the need for a physical release. This is what he had been waiting for. This was his moment to turn the tables.

"I am a man with feelings, hopes, fears, and desires of my own. I am not going to allow you to use me as your personal sex toy and discard me when you are finished." He watched Savannah's jaw drop. But he had a few more nails in his pocket. He pulled back his arm and allowed the hammer to fall.

"If you want any more of this ..." his hand made a circular motion around his crotch, "... you are going to have to give me something in return." To irritate her beyond measure, he gripped himself showing her the outline. "If you want some of this love, you will have to let go of your bullshit ideas and love the whole man. If not, we can just be friends and spend wonderful evenings together like tonight." *Bishop to Queen Three ... Check.*

He opened the door and walked out. "Good night, my lovely friend. You have the number."

Bishop to Knight Three ... Checkmate.

She was fit to be tied. Of all the cockamamie nerve! Now, she was pissed, frustrated, and hornier than ever. She grabbed her keys and headed to Darwin's. He answered the door, concerned that something was wrong since it was midnight. She stomped past him and headed straight to his bedroom. He joined her there seconds later. "You want to know how I like it, let me show you." She pushed him back on the bed, worked him up with her mouth and climbed aboard. Each time Darwin got close, she would unhinge the two of them and straddle his face, bringing her closer to her finish. Finally, when she was ready, she slid over him, and rode him to the finale. She held nothing back as she gyrated, pulsated, and milked him of everything he had. Her clothing had not been removed, but she righted herself, telling him goodnight as she pulled the covers over him.

It still was not even close to the level of what she had with Jesse. Fine! He wanted emotion and love? She would give it to him by the bucket. She had held back so much over the last three years. If Jesse wanted it, she would let him have it. Love him back? He was going to regret this request. She sent him a text.

Jesse arrived at her apartment at six on the dot. Although his birthday wasn't for a few more days, he was happy she had remembered. Savannah instructed him to go and wash the day off him. In the guest bathroom, he found a change of clothing and a fishing magazine. Showered, shaved, and dressed, he walked down the stairs and stared at her. Jesse felt she was up to something.

"You look very handsome," she told him as she straightened his collar. "Are you ready to roll?"

He wore dark grey slacks, a cerulean blue shirt, and a pair of open toe gray men's leather slides, an entire outfit she had purchased for him. Jesse looked down at his feet with a scrunched face. "How did you know what size shoes or *sandals*?"

"Your feet need to breath. You always wear closed in shoes, it is not healthy for the skin on your feet," she explained as she extended her arm to demonstrate how she measured his shoe size.

Smart.

"And how did you know what size pants and shirt to buy?"

A coy smile crossed her lips as she sat on the couch. "I told the guy in the store your waist was about this big." She spread her legs in her skirt, indicating how wide her legs had to go to accommodate him.

"You did not!" Jesse said incredulously.

Savannah rose from the couch and kicked off her high-heeled sandals. "Yes, I did. I also told him that in stocking feet, your belt buckle hit me here." She pointed to her midsection, just below her navel. "He knew how long the pants had to be, but I told him you had large, powerful thighs so we went up a size." As she said the word thighs, her fingers grazed over his.

"The shirt was easy. You fit in my brother's tee, so I called him and asked what size he wore and went up one." She grabbed her keys and the door handle, slipping back into her shoes ushering him out to the parking garage. "Do you like the color of the shirt?"

"It is an odd color blue, but I like it," he said as she unlocked the doors to her car. Jesse slid into the passenger seat and felt like a sardine. Savannah reached between his legs and adjusted the seat handle, giving him more legroom.

"The blue of the shirt is almost the same color of your eyes, when you are really turned on," she said as she pulled away from the parking space. *Like they are now.*

She was playing dirty and he loved it. "So with my blue eyes and your brown ones ..." he paused for a minute to get her brain moving. "... what color would our children's eyes be?"

Savannah did not miss a beat. "Well brown is the dominant color, in all honesty, and since blue is the recessive trait, there is a 50/50 chance the child could have either." She drove down the main road, coming up by the Civic Center and entering I-20 headed East.

"It would be really cool if we had a little girl and she had hazel eyes," Jesse said. "I would love to name her Sahara."

Her eyes remained fixed on the road, as she searched for the right thing to say next, but instead he piped up, "You know the timing belt is about to go on this car, it need struts, and the alignment is off."

"I am aware," she told him. "I will get it fixed next

month."

"Why?" He tried to turn in the seat, but there was very little room for him to move. "The timing belt and labor will cost more than the car is worth."

"What do you suggest I do, Mr. Mechanic?"

Jesse stared out the window. "If it dies before you are ready to get something else, I will loan you my Cherokee. I hardly ever drive it."

It was a quiet dinner. As they enjoyed their meal, they talked about furniture and fishing. For his birthday, she gave him a new tackle box, which surprised him. Savannah had listened to what he told her about fishing on the weekends with his father and the type of lures he used.

Savannah was showing that she cared deeply for him. She spent money on him while knowing her car needed to be fixed. His chest swelled, filling him with pride at having pushed the lady to give something back.

She dropped him at his at his truck, saying good night with a brief kiss on his lips.

Savannah was learning to love him.

It was the best birthday present a man could receive.

Chapter Twenty

September

In church on Sunday, Darwin continued to cast speculative glances her way. They had an early supper at her mother's house and he seemed almost uncomfortable with his fiancée. Her mother picked up on the trouble right away. Emurial Niden asked her to stay and leaned toward Darwin to give him a hug. "I'll drive her home."

Emurial was concerned that Darwin was way too eager to get away. The table hadn't even been cleared when her mother turned and asked, "What is his name and what have you done?"

Savannah collected the dirty plates. "What makes you think I've done something?"

Emurial was not about to mince words with her daughter. "I know that look and you unleashed something on him that he cannot wrap his mind around. Did you bring another dog's tricks into that man's yard?"

This was boring her. The whole scenario was boring her. Lying was boring her and she just wanted to be herself. "Seriously, Mother, stop being so dramatic. If Darwin wants to run with the big dogs, he has to stop pissing like a pup." That was all she had to say on the matter.

The rest of it was none of her mother's business.

Thursday

As the evening arrived, she made meatloaf, sour cream

mashed potatoes, haricot verts, and a sweet potato pie. Instead of slutty clothing, she wore a simple skirt, a modest blouse, and a push-up bra. Her thick black hair that she often wore pulled back into a ponytail was piled high upon her head, with loose tendrils framing her face and her neck. She made a pitcher of grape Kool-Aid with slices of lemons, and when the door opened at 6 pm, she greeted Jesse at the door with a cold glass.

"Good evening, Baby. How has your week been?" she asked him as she made her way back to the kitchen to check on the pie.

Slowly, as if uncertain of his standing, he rounded the corner to spot the meatloaf and his eyes got wide. When she pulled the sweet potato pie from the oven and place it on the cooling racks, he sat down the glass and walked up behind her embracing her from behind, nearly squeezing the life out of her.

"Oh God, Savannah..." She pried his fingers loose so she could turn and face him. His eyes were brimming with emotion and tears. The feeling was mutual. "I have missed you so much, Baby." He kissed her face, her neck, and her jawline. "Tell me how much you missed me, too."

She kissed him back, pushing him toward the couch. She needed Jesse in a way that could only connect two souls into a single moment. She grabbed his bag and removed the necessary tools, as he tilled away in her womanhood with his fingers. "I missed you, too, Jesse," she told him as his fingers plunged deep and she cried out. She yanked her blouse over her head, not bothering to unfasten her bra as she lifted the cups over her mounds to expose her breast. She shoved them in his face, then his mouth, commanding him, "Suck them!"

Jesse's teeth grazed across the nipples as his thumb massaged the nub of flesh and his fingers worked in and out of her valley.

Savannah took the condom from his hand and ripped open the package, but before she placed it upon him, she disengaged from his hand, dropped to her knees and for the first time, took him into her mouth. Clean, dirty, or slightly tart, she didn't care. His head flopped back on the couch, his mouth form an 'O' as he tried to catch his breath. She was going to unleash every tool she had at her disposal on him. She sucked hard, stroking, massaging, and pleasing him.

She applied the protection, slid her underwear to the side and straddled his hips. Slowly, inch-by-inch, she took him in. Her breasts were shoved in his face and once she was seated, she slid back and slammed full force into him. "You like this, Tool Boy?" She asked as she rocked her pelvis back and forth.

"Does this feel good to you, Jesse?" she asked as she picked up her pace. He only mumbled as his eyes rolled upward and his breathing became erratic. "Look at me, and tell me, Jesse. Tell me what you've been wanting to say."

She gripped the back of the couch using it for leverage. He felt so damned good she could not get enough of him. She picked up her pace. She used her abdominal muscles, her pelvic muscles and her thigh muscles to give him what she had been holding on to for a month. The force of their movements was so great that the couch began to shift and move across the floor. They became verbal and extra noisy. As he bit down on her nipple, she yelled at him, "Say it! Tell me!"

As Jesse neared his climax, he held onto her hips, pulling and pushing her, thrusting his hips upward, and calling her name between gritted teeth he mumbled, "You feel so fucking good." He quickly turned over, ending up on his back, holding her hips in his hands. He began to raise and lift her over his need until he too was losing control. "Say it, Jesse. Tell me!" The start of her climax nearly paralyzed him it was so intense. He was panting, trying to hold off as he flexed his stomach muscles to stave off his release, but it was too much. He wrapped his arms around her waist and reversed their positions on the couch.

He withdrew and shoved himself into her. She cried out his name. He lunged into her again and again and again. The waves of her orgasm washed over her as she lay still. He called her name, "Savannah." His eyes were heavy with passion as she looked up at him, "I love you so much. Every moment with you is magical." He began to move slowly within her.

He did not enter the vortex with her, but was waiting for the one thing he needed to hear. "Jesse, I love you, too."

"Savannah," he whispered as he picked up his rhythm. "Say it again. Tell me again, my Lovely, tell me," he said as he moved inside of her.

"I love you, Jesse. Fill me up, Jesse, give me all of you and give me everything you have." He cried out her name as the force of his thrusting moved the couch closer to the kitchen.

They collapsed on the sofa, laughing when they noticed the couch's proximity to the stove. Jesse shifted his weight so he wouldn't crush her. "So much for an English sofa on casters."

"I am more worried that my neighbors heard us." She laughed as she planted loving kisses on his face.

Those two items were the least of their worries. Jesse had forgotten to lock the front door. The unexpected guest, who heard the commotion, had slowly peered inside and then eased back out, not calling attention to his presence.

Chapter Twenty - One

Darwin was having trouble finding a way to start the conversation to address what Savannah had unleashed on him that late night. He was concerned that in two years, he had never seen that side of her. What troubled him more than anything else was his inability to please her. Several times she had stopped to increase his staying power and he had failed miserably to meet or match her drive.

In his mind, he realized that Savannah was a ten, but what made her so amazing was she thought she was a six. On any scale, from a good side, or right angle, he understood his lot in life. He would never surpass the threshold of a seven, even if he spent six days a week in the gym. Unfortunately, his shortcomings were not balanced out with his ability to perform in bed. Even as a black man, he was not gifted with a large endowment. It was average.

His former lovers, if they could be called that, deemed him a shallow, self-centered asshole. He had felt safe with Savannah because she was non-judgmental. His forehead throbbed as he thought of the number of times she had lain under him, allowing him to finish, now knowing that she was left unsatisfied. A feeling of inadequacy threatened to overrun him, with the idea that a life of not satisfying her in bed would eventually ruin the marriage.

An image of the muscle-bound Jesse flashed through his psyche.

He had not been wrong. Somebody, if not that mother cocker, was teaching his sweet angel how to be nasty. He didn't like it, not one bit. He decided to bring it up to her over dinner. "Savannah, I understand your taste is a tad bit different from mine and if you have been unfaithful to me in order to become ..." he cleared his throat. "... more fulfilled, I can understand."

Savannah's jaw was agape with a piece of beef dangling between her lips. Darwin asked the question that Jesse, her mother, and her brother, Jerwane, had also asked, "Why are you marrying me?"

She shoveled meat into her mouth. "Because, I love you, Darwin." He smiled at her but was not ready to let the subject drop.

"But are you *in* love with me?" he asked as he looked over the glass of Merlot.

"Darwin, love is not quantifiable and very seldom qualifiable. People rant on and on about what they think love is and whom they are in love with, but it is all bullshit." She sipped her glass of wine. She was tired of having this conversation. First with Jesse and now with him. *When did men become so sappy? Had the testosterone been bred out of them, replacing the American man with a whipped Mama's boy who needed to discuss his feelings?*

"Being *in* love does not pay the bills, feed and clothe the kids, or provide longevity in marriage. Those things are done through logic, understanding, and nurturing one another," she told him with more than a mere annoyance.

Darwin smiled at her. She had inadvertently answered his question. She was not in love with him, but marrying him for security.

She had been candid with him, so he would do the same with her. "Whoever he is—and I don't need to know—he has to go. You will not share my bed for a roof over your head then crawl into his for recreation."

Savannah looked at Darwin with sharp eyes. "Considering the roof I have over my head now is not by your hand, but my own, I think I am capable of maintaining it if need be. And the same thing goes for you. If you have something on the side, she will need to be set free."

It was out in the air. The soon to be Mr. and Mrs. Finney stared at each other. "You have until December to clean your house before you move into mine and become Mrs. Finney."

Savannah was nonplussed, as she gave back as good as she got, "And you have until December to be better, Mr. Finney." It was not implied, nor stated what he needed to be better at. As far as she was concerned the list had about ten items and stingy was at the top.

This was turning out to be one of the best months of Savannah Niden's life. Her articles, which had been submitted to several publications earlier in the year, were all accepted, including one in an NIH journal and another in the *Journal of Biological Chemistry* on mitochondrial oxidation. Although much of her research focused on high blood pressure, some of her findings were easily correlated to oxygen deficiency in red blood cells in hypertensive patients and diabetics. This was a proud moment.

She was even more proud when the Dean informed her that she had made Assistant Professor. It would not be official for two months, but it also came with a pay increase. It was a raise that would afford her some breathing room. The new position meant more classes to teach, more research to study, and more grants to write, but she was relishing in the new options for her workday. This was an extremely happy moment and she hoped everyone would be joyful for her.

Her soon-to-be-husband was not. When she shared her great news with Darwin, he congratulated her with what bordered on insincere praise, "That's wonderful, Darling, but I was hoping we would be starting a family in the latter part of the year." *This bullheaded man is not going to ruin my shining moment.* She called Jesse, who, on Thursday evening, arrived with flowers and a bottle of champagne to celebrate. When she told him about her new responsibilities, he hugged her and congratulated her again. He had a question, and Savannah held her breath.

"I may not make six figures, but I do pretty well. Do you think with your pay raise that our combined incomes can get you that fancy car and the house you want in Vestavia Hills?"

She smiled at his insightfulness, but she was in a new frame of mind as well. "Or, I can stay right here and get a new Ford." Her thought patterns were changing. She was finding out what she really liked and maybe, just maybe, she wasn't ready to be anyone's trophy wife.

Jesse understood what she was feeling, but escapism wasn't an option this time. He wanted to know. "How long have you been engaged to Darwin?"

Savannah, who was sitting next to him on the couch, cradled in the crook of his arm, looked at him, realizing, but not rationalizing something that had been niggling in the back of her mind for some time. "I actually got engaged to him on Valentine's night, an hour before I met you."

Their eyes met. Jesse held the gaze. Maybe Big Sam had been right all along and timing was everything. She wasn't married yet. Instead of capitalizing on this small victory of self-doubt slithering through her mind, he opted instead to take the high road. "Interesting."

Then he changed the subject. "That sweet potato pie was fantastic. Can I bribe you to make another one day?"

The kudzu had taken root, now it was time to increase the fertilizing schedule.

Chapter Twenty-Two ♡

<u>October</u>

It was a fantastic Friday morning. Jesse showered and put on a loose fitting pair of hot red boxer briefs. He had a craving for coffee. He began whistling as he headed down the stairs to start a pot of the dark brew that would pair nicely with a couple of boiled eggs and a few slices of bacon for breakfast. It amazed him that after nine months of making love to Savannah it was just as exciting as it was the first time. Although he wasn't a singer, this morning his heart was melodic as he began belting out a Tim McGraw song.

He rounded the corner to the kitchen and stopped short when he spotted an unfamiliar large black man standing in Savannah's kitchen. The man was in the fridge and Jesse's emotions were going haywire. *This dude had better not be Friday showing up early!* The man turned around, eyeing Jesse, taking everything in, especially his lack of clothing. Thank goodness he had opted for the underwear! Jesse noticed his hair, the skin coloring, nose, and mouth. "Oh, you must be Savannah's brother."

Jerwane was still staring. "Yes, and that would make you her … what?"

Jesse could not help himself as he headed for the cabinet to get the coffee. "I am her maintenance man."

Jerwane closed the fridge and found himself staring at the half naked white man in his sister's kitchen. "You do know you have a short contract on this lease, right?"

"Not if I'm planning to relocate her to another facility." He smiled at Jerwane as he started the coffee. Her brother was now leaning against the fridge, leaving Jesse with a waning appetite.

"Funny, Mr. Rogers, but I think you are in the wrong neighborhood," he said defensively. This was not her brother's call, nor was it his business, and Jesse was not going to engage him any further. Savannah arrived in the kitchen with a smile on her face, fully dressed and ready to raid the fridge. After last night, she was starving. She told her brother good morning, kissed him on the cheek, and pushed him out of the way as she began to make lunch bags. As large as the man was, he was putty in his little sister's hands.

Jesse broke the awkward silence. "I started coffee, but not breakfast. I think I'm going to bypass it this morning."

She turned as if she had been struck across the face with a hot a stick. "Seriously? You know it is the only way to start off the day." Jesse raised his eyebrows, licked his bottom lip, and stretched high to the ceiling.

Savannah understood his unspoken words. "You are lucky my brother is in this kitchen!"

"And if he wasn't?" Jesse asked as he moved closer to the center of the room. Savannah moved closer to him as well. They stood toe-to-toe in the center of the floor, as if they were in a Mexican standoff, "What would you do, Science Girl?"

Savannah poked him in the belly with her index finger. "I would ride you so hard I would scramble your molecules."

Jerwane's mouth opened, his lips curling downward as if he had just eaten some bad fish, as he silently mouthed the word, "Eeeewwwww!"

"I love it when you talk that science talk, Baby, give me some more," Jesse said as he wrapped his arms around her waist.

She wrapped her arms around his neck, her lips slowly mouthing the words, "Deoxyribonucleic acid!"

Jesse shrugged his shoulders as though he were chilled. "Oohh, not the DNA!"

Savannah wiggled her hips against Jesse's, making suggestive bumps with each of the following words, "Polymerase chain reaction."

Jesse buckled at the knees. "Oh yeah, amplify that DNA, Baby!"

She raised her leg and wrapped it around his waist. "Mitochondrial oxidative phosphorylation."

"Oh hell, that did it, you are in trouble now." He hoisted a giggling Savannah over his shoulder, swatting her on the ass, but as he turned he remembered her brother was standing there. Jerwane's face was further contorted as if he had walked in on their parents going at it. The poor guy looked traumatized. Jesse lowered Savannah back to the floor, kissed her lightly on the lips, and excused himself to go and get dressed.

"Ooooh, coffee's ready, Jesse," she yelled up the stairs at her maintenance man as she poured a cup for herself and offered her brother one as well. Jerwane refused. He wanted to say something, but was not sure what. His main concern was tamping down the bile that was creeping up his esophagus. Savannah reached for him and mushed his face, trying to reset his facial expression. When she could not straighten his face, she went for the leftovers to finish the lunch bags.

Jesse returned a few minutes later, pants on and buttoning a long-sleeved Montgomery Construction shirt. The logo was not wasted on Jerwane. When he factored in Darwin's new assignment, plus a half-naked white dude who worked at the same company, it was adding up to a hot mess. What was his sister doing?

Savannah handed Jesse the cup of coffee and a kiss. "I will see you next week."

"Change of location I'm afraid, we are headed to a new facility next week," Jesse told her as he looked over Savannah's shoulder at her brother, while he accepted her help stuffing the tails of his shirt down his pants. He pulled a plane ticket out of his back pocket. "I'm leaving for the Builders' Convention in Colorado Springs on Sunday. Here's your ticket. You're on the 6 pm Wednesday night."

Savannah accepted the ticket and began to think of the numerous vacation days she had yet to use. She was going away with Jesse! She glazed over during the remainder of his instructions. He said something about a cab to the hotel, then something about the folder he stuck in her hand, plus the envelope with a check. *Do I need to pay his bills while he is gone?*

Hold on! I am going away with Jesse!

"Savannah, I'm not sure if it is enough, my sister said it should be." He was still saying something with that sexy mouth. It was too late for her; she was going all goo-goo.

Wait! I am going away with Jesse!

Jesse pinched her arm. "Science Girl, this is important. You will need a conservative crimson-colored cocktail dress for Thursday night, a conservative black cocktail dress for Friday night, and a tasteful swimsuit for the

135

pool party on Saturday. It'll be chilly, so you will need some kind of wrap thing. I think that's what Mary Kate said."

She nodded and glanced at the envelope. "Whoa, there is a thousand dollar check in here.... Who is Mary Kate?"

"My sister. She said it should be more than enough for two dresses and a swimsuit. Do you think you will need more?"

Savannah shook her head no, wondering where in the hell his sister liked to shop.

"Great, I will see you on Wednesday night." He pulled her into his arms and kissed her deeply. "I love you so much, I wish you could leave with me."

When Savannah caught her breath, she huskily whispered, "I will see you in Colorado next week."

Jesse reached for his lunch and was surprised when Savannah handed him a new blue Igloo lunch cooler. "This is so much better than a brown bag. It'll keep your coffee hot and food cool."

"This is nice, thank you, my Lovely." Jesse accepted his lunch and stepped back. "Jerwane, it was nice to meet you."

Her brother, who was still in six levels of shock, in dire need of vomiting, and whose face was statically contorted, replied, "Nice to meet me? We were never introduced! I don't even know your damn name, Man!"

Jesse extended his hand. "Jesse." Jerwane accepted it with some reluctance. One last look at Savannah and he wanted her to say it in front of her brother, "Send me off with a smile."

"Love me some of you, Jesse," she said. It wasn't good enough for him. He needed her brother to hear the words from her lips.

He stepped back inside, gathered her in his arms again. "Savanah, I can never get tired of hearing you say it. Tell me again."

"I love you, Jesse." She kissed him fully on the mouth.

"I love you back, Science Girl." As he released her beautiful body, he tilted his head to Jerwane. "If anything should change, you have the number." And with that, he was gone.

Savannah checked her watch. She was going to be late. She kissed Jerwane on the cheek once more. "Good seeing you." Then she thought about it. "Wait a minute. Why are you here anyway?"

"I came to talk to you about leaving your door open at night, Button Nose. If I walked in and saw what I saw, what is to stop Darwin?"

Savannah stopped short. He always called her Button Nose when he was about to deliver bad news. She wasn't sure what he had seen but really didn't give a flying pail of fermented feces. This was her life.

With a shrug of her shoulders, she replied, "Well, remember to lock it on your way out." She grabbed her lunch and headed off to work. She was going away for a weekend with Jesse to Colorado Springs and she was going to get initiated into the mile high club, literally. It had been a long time since she was this happy. Her elation could barely be contained. It set so well into her soul that she wanted to start cursing at random people for no reason, like a crazy person.

What the heck! "Hey, Jerwane, happy fucking Friday!"

She burst into a maniacal laugh as she let herself out the front door and made her way to the car. She had so much to do and so little time that she started a mental list. First things first: this weekend she was shopping! Shucks, maybe there was something to this love stuff after all.

Chapter Twenty-Three

Wednesday

Savannah was excited as she closed out the final experiments before leaving the lab. In the hall, two frantic students worried over grades stopped her. She referred them to the departmental secretary and told them to set up an appointment with her next week. Her mind was somewhere else. She had never been away with a man for a weekend trip before. Sure, there had been a surprise romantic night at the Holiday Inn one evening, but a plane ticket to a resort? This was different. It was very nice that Jesse also provided her with some pocket money to shop for the things she needed. The crimson dress and the black dress she found on sale at Burlington. The swimsuit she had gotten off a clearance rack at Parisian's as well as a few items for the cooler temps in October in the mountains.

Last night, she could not hide her enthusiasm and the sheer glee in her spirit when she had dinner with Darwin, who sulked the whole night. First, there was something wrong with the project. The job was much more detailed than he initially thought. Then, he complained that the customers were very picky and driving him insane with their changes. "The difference between ecru and beige is so subtle, who gives a dancing paint bucket about the color of a single wall? Beige is not an accent color!" Even his griping and whelping wouldn't bring her down.

"Darwin," she said as she sliced through the chops his

139

housekeeper had overcooked. "You said this was your opportunity to move your career up a level, correct?" He nodded with some uncertainty, but she continued with a smile. "The powers that be at Montgomery Construction awarded the contract to Green & Associates, naming you as the Project Lead. They have confidence in your ability and so do I. You can do this. I know you can. Remember the bigger picture."

He seemed to be placated and Savannah was still cheerful. She didn't understand Darwin sometimes. When the things he wanted and hoped for were awarded to him, he often complained or found fallacy with them. Savannah pondered the idea that maybe once they were married, their relationship would follow the same pattern.

By the time Jerwane drove her to the airport on Wednesday night, she was over her self-doubts. She was on her way to Colorado Springs for some alone and away time with a man she found herself enjoying far more than she should. She wasn't stupid. She fully understood that a cold beer always tasted better from someone else's mug and Jesse had a big frosty tankard. She loved that tankard and she loved the man.

Part of her excitement resided in the idea this would be the first time they could be out in the open, versus the few hours alone behind closed doors or a dinner and movie in a dark corner. It would also be the first time she had an opportunity to see Jesse in his element and for her, it was important to see how he interacted with other people. She knew how he treated her, but how was he with others?

Jerwane interrupted her thoughts, "Savannah, you do realize in this scenario, you are the bad guy."

Brows furrowed and totally confused, she looked at her

brother as if he had colored flatulence emanating from his ass. "What are you talking about, Jerwane?"

"Most women would love to have a good man. You obviously have two and are playing them both. Button Nose, *you* are the bad guy."

As they stood on the sidewalk at the entrance to the airport terminal, Jerwane looked at his younger sibling with a bit of distaste in his mouth. Savannah was not going to allow him to control this moment of freedom for her. It seemed no matter what she did, no one wanted her to be happy. They just wanted to control her. The time had arrived for it all to stop.

"How dare you judge me when you have had women going out the back door while another was coming in the front!" His eyebrows popped up. "Your nasty ass didn't even bother to change the sheets before you plopped another young body in the wet mess from the first one."

"So, you changing the sheets in between dick rides makes it okay?"

Savannah slapped his face. "Darwin does not stay at my place, only Jesse. I love them both in different ways, Jerwane. I am just making sure that when I get married next year that I have not missed out on something. If that makes me a whore or the bad guy in your eyes, then fine!"

He dropped his head and rubbed his stinging cheek. "I am not saying you are a whore, Button Nose, I am just saying ..." he paused looking for the right words, his hands pointing up and down at her body "... this isn't you."

Life was too short to be bridled and miserable. She was joyful and her big brother was not going to spoil it for her. It was time for him to see his little sister in a new light.

"Well whoever is in this body is headed to Colorado Springs for four days of dick riding." She threw up two fingers, yelled deuces, and disappeared through the terminal doors.

It was a relaxed flight from Birmingham, changing planes in Dallas, then on to Colorado, arriving at 10 pm. She traveled light with a carry-on bag and reached the sidewalk in Colorado Springs at 10:20. Hailing a cab was easy. She arrived at the Broadmoor Hotel & Resort at almost 11 pm. She was weary, but not worn. A hot shower and something to nosh on would snap her back to a sexy mood. At the counter, she stated her name and said there was a package for her. The desk clerk handed it over, along with an envelope that held a room key. An attendant escorted her to the west tower patio suites where their room was located.

Savannah slipped the key into the door, walked inside, and set her bag beside the entrance as she inhaled the fragrance of the room. Candles were burning, soft music was playing, and rose petals made a trail on the floor. Her toes sank into the deep pile of the luxurious carpet as she followed the petals to the main bedroom surprised when Jesse was not waiting for her in the bed, but the petals continued on into the bathroom. She removed her shoes at the door as she tiptoed around the corner to see a massive garden-size tub, filled with bubbles. Jesse stood at the side of the tub with a glass of wine wearing nothing but a towel and a large smile.. "I thought you would never get here."

Those were the last words he spoke as he helped her disrobe and climb into the tub of warm water. He dropped in a lemongrass bath seed from the Pilgrim Soap

Company, making a point to show it off. *Thoughtful*. He scrubbed her back and the soles of her feet and massaged her shoulders. Savannah used the large bath sponge to wash every inch of his body as they relaxed in the quiet moments of togetherness before turning in for the night.

Wrapped in a fluffy hotel bathrobe, Savannah sat on the patio staring at the mountains. The view of the lake was equally as breathtaking as she listened to Jesse direct the room service assistant to where she sat. Breakfast looked delicious and it was nice to be on a mini vacation. Savannah had never been on a real vacation before. Of course, there had been some travel in her life, mostly to conferences, but to get away to a magnificent place like this was a blessing. The suite was luxurious, the overstuffed furniture was grand, and her roommate was a sexual dynamo. In her mind, the nagging thought of the hour window between agreeing to be Mrs. Finney and meeting Jesse was bugging her a bit. If she had met Jesse two hours before she got engaged, versus two hours after, maybe she would not be a cheating *dick rider* in her brother's eyes.

A feathery light kiss landed on her lips as Jesse slipped into the chair beside her to be served his breakfast. He tipped the waiter and then handed his companion a Montgomery Construction folder. "Inside, you will find your itinerary and all relevant info about the conference including the evening events and scheduled activities if you wish to take part."

Over her coffee mug, wide eyes stared at him. "I have an itinerary?"

"Yes, after breakfast, you have an appointment at the spa and then I would love for you to meet me for lunch." He told her of a local hot spot he really wanted to take her to. "Then you are free for a few hours to read, golf, or do whatever you want." He loaded in a mouthful of eggs. "Tonight is the Crimson and Black Gala."

The only thing Savannah heard was spa. She had never been to one and was excited. One of the first things Jesse had noticed when she walked into the bathroom was her hands. They were blissfully ring-free, as per their agreement. He needed to change that. "Oh, I almost forgot." He stood and disappeared into the bathroom, returning minutes later.

A small velvet box was placed on the table, next to her coffee cup. Savannah was almost afraid to open it. "I know your birthday is in two weeks, but I wanted to give this to you now."

Her hands were shaking as she reached for the container. Tentative fingers opened the case to reveal the most stunning topaz ring she ever laid eyes upon. It wasn't too big, it wasn't too flashy, and it was subtly grand. "Here," he said. "Allow me." He removed the emerald cut, two-carat ring from the box and slipped it on her left ring finger. A perfect fit. The ceremonious move was followed by a passionate kiss and words that knotted her stomach. "I could spend the rest of my life waking up with you, Savannah Niden."

He quickly checked his watch. "Ooh, I can't be late. I'm teaching this morning. Enjoy your day, Science Girl." As she sat on the patio, twirling with raw emotion, Jesse was dressed and headed out the door in less than five minutes. Jesse gave her another brief kiss, adding, "I will meet you at the front desk at noon."

Savannah had been played.

She was now engaged to two men and Jesse had made his move to make her choose.

Chapter Twenty-Four

The Broadmoor Hotel was beautiful. There were amenities and features at this hotel that Savannah had heard of, but never actually experienced. This was a whole new world to her. She began to think of ways she could save money to afford some weekend getaways with the girls. It would be nice to hang out here with Traci and Sheryl. She stopped. *Was it a Freudian mind hump that I did not think about bringing Darwin to a place like this?*

Her private tour of a new mental future ended when she arrived at the spa doors. Today, she had chosen to wear simple khakis with a soft pink long-sleeved sweater set and some loafers. A delicate strand of freshwater pearls was hanging from her neck along with matching teardrop pearl earrings. Inside the spa, the lavender scents immediately brought her to a relaxed mental frame of mind and she was anxious to see what Jesse had picked out for her pampering session.

The foyer was empty sans one lady who appeared to be the same age as Savannah, with long, deep black hair and equally intense blue eyes. Savannah smiled at her and said good morning. The lady didn't smile back, but looked toward the door as if she was waiting, very impatiently, for someone to join her.

The pretty blond behind the counter asked Savannah, "Good Morning, may I help **you?**"

"Yes. I am Dr. Savannah Niden. I have a 9:30 appointment I believe." She heard the black haired woman sputter whatever she was drinking and begin to choke. Savannah and the associate both rushed to the woman's side, with Savannah being the first to speak. "Are you okay?"

Amidst watery eyes and coughs, the lady uprighted herself, allowing Savannah to rejoin the attendant back at the counter. The young girl added, "Okay, Dr. Niden, you have been scheduled for a couple's massage. I think yours is a Swedish massage."

Savannah interrupted the young woman, "I am sorry, but did you say couple's massage? There must be some misunderstanding."

The dark haired woman with blue eyes stepped forward. "No, I am your partner for today." Savannah and the woman both stared at her. "I am Mary Kate, Jesse's sister." She extended her hand.

Play it cool, girl. Play it cool. Instead of taking her hand for a shake, Savannah stepped forward and embraced his sister. "It is great to meet you." She would not lie and say *Jesse has told me so much about you*, because he had only mentioned he had a brother and a sister, and that was Mary Kate's suggestions for shopping, nothing more. "Forgive me for hugging you, but I figured the spa was your idea."

"Actually, no, it was Jesse's." She took the robe the attendant handed her and both ladies followed the girl down the hall. "It appears he would like us to get to know each other better."

An ice-cold chill coursed through Savannah's veins as she realized Jesse had also not described her to his sister, leaving out a very important detail. She would fill in the holes and ease the awkwardness between them if she could. "I guess Jesse failed to mention an important detail about me," she said as she tried to gauge the sister's reaction. "Most people are really shocked when they find out that I am a doctor. Even more so when they find out I am a doctor of letters and a researcher."

Mary Kate was now paying attention. "So you are an MD and a Ph.D.?" She asked as she secured her purse in the cabinet and Savannah did the same.

"No, just a Ph.D. and assistant professor at UAB," she said as she removed her shoes.

"What do you research?" Mary Kate asked as she placed her shoes in the bottom of the locker.

Savannah was reluctant to say, but she wanted to make a good impression and break the ice. "High blood pressure as well as the metabolic disorders in the modulation of mitochondrial protein phosphorylation by soluble adenylyl cyclase that ameliorates cytochrome oxidase defects in African Americans."

Mary Kate glazed over, but had to ask, "Who the hell is suffering from that? What the hell is that?"

She and Savannah both began to laugh. The icebreaker had worked. Mary Kate was a rather pretty woman, standing at five feet eight, with much of the same patrician features as Jesse and a full mouth and eyes that bore into a person's soul. Savannah wasn't bashful as she stripped down to her bra and panties and was grateful she had put on a matching set.

Mary Kate's breath caught. "Dear Heavens, you have an amazing body!" Savannah looked down to see what she was talking about. "You must live in the gym."

"On the contrary, I do Zumba on Monday and Wednesday nights on campus, and watch what I eat." Mary Kate was moving uncomfortably close to her and pointed at her breasts.

"Do you mind?"

Do I mind what? Savannah was now really uncomfortable, but went with it. "No, go ahead."

In the middle of the room, Mary Kate cupped her breast and began to squeeze the mounds. Their massage therapists chose that exact moment to walk into the room, only to beg forgiveness and back out. "Oh my goodness, they are real!" It got weirder from there as Mary Kate felt her skin, tested to see if her ass was real, then actually ran her hands through her hair.

Savannah had enough, "Mary Kate, I am a real girl, please stop checking for attachments and add-ons. If you continue to feel me up, you are at least going to have to ask me to dance or buy me a drink." Jesse's sister began to blush, feeling stupid, and apologized profusely. They laughed some more as they headed into the massage room to begin their pampering session.

They remained quiet and said little as the very large women rubbed, patted and massaged their tired, achy muscles and increased their blood circulation. It felt wonderful. An hour and ten minutes later, she and Mary Kate sat in the whirlpool, where she noticed the ring on Savannah's finger. Savannah told her the same thing Jesse had shared. "It is an early birthday present." She left it there and said no more.

They chatted a bit more before heading to the aromatherapy room. It became obvious to Mary Kate that Savannah didn't know her brother's role at Montgomery Construction. She did share that she worked in the accounting department and handled most of Jesse's accounts. Thoughts flooded Savannah's mind about nepotism, but it worked for them, which reminded her. "Oh, thank you for the check for my supplies for this trip ..." she paused and looked at the sister. "... I have the receipts and can write you a check to return what I didn't spend."

Mary Kate was surprised that she had not spent it all and was willing to give back what she had not used. Jesse's sister rose and walked over to Savannah and hugged her. "I like you, Doc. I can see why he does as well."

"I like you, too, Mary Kate," she added with some hesitation. "I always wondered what it would be like to have a sister. You seem like you are a really cool one."

May Kate blushed a bit, "Yep, you can't get much cooler than me."

They were still laughing as they dressed and headed to the lobby a little bit before noon. Jesse looked up to see them coming, walking arm in arm like high school pals. He knew his sister was going to love Savannah as much as he did and he thought he would invite Mary Kate to join them for lunch, but she declined, insisting she had paperwork to process.

A quick hug and kiss and she was off. Savannah turned to see her hunky lover watching her and smiled, "I'm starving, where we are headed?"

After lunch, Savannah filled her afternoon with a walk around the property grounds. She ran into a nice gentleman with a deep Southern accent who asked her to join him for coffee. He said people called him Big Sam.

Over sweet rolls and bad jokes, Savannah spent nearly three hours lost in conversation with the hazel eyed, gray haired gentleman, discussing everything from furniture making to baby raising. The loss of time was troubling as it lessened her time to get dressed for the gala. Big Sam had been so warm and cordial that she found herself giving him a big hug and a kiss on the cheek as she excused herself to prepare for the gala. She confessed her nervousness in her dress choice, adding, "I hope my guy likes what I'm wearing."

Big Sam hugged her briefly. "I'm certain you'll make very few choices that your young man would disagree with young lady."

She patted his hands and took off to the suite. Jesse was already in the shower, so she stripped down and decided to join him for a quick wash. They both dressed quickly and Savannah's breath caught when Jesse walked out in the black suit, crimson shirt, and black tie. "Wow, you clean up nice."

Savannah didn't look like a slouch herself in the asymmetrical, one sleeved rayon dress, which highlighted her toned arms and small waist and clung to her hips in all the right places. Jesse stood there for a minute transfixed. The loose curls that framed her face added a softness to her eyes that were highlighted with just a touch of mascara, some body dust on her cheeks, and hint of color to her lips. She was flawless. Jesse found his body reacting and wanting her right now.

"Damn," he said reaching for her.

Savannah held up her hand. "Don't even think about it. I am not going to anyone's function smelling like I have been ridden hard and put away wet. Literally. You are going to have to wait."

Although he was pouting, he extended his arm and escorted her to the ballroom. There were so many people mixing and mingling. She immediately spotted Mary Kate and waved to her. She heard a boisterous laugh and noticed Big Sam, who turned to look at them. Savannah turned to Jesse, "Hey, I want to introduce you to someone I met today." She drug him by the arm across the room.

It was genuine affection when she greeted Big Sam who complimented her on the dress choice before placing a kiss on her cheek. "Jesse, this is Big Sam." She beamed at Jesse, who stepped forward and embraced the man who was only a couple of inches taller than him.

"What time did you guys make it in?" Jesse asked him.

Big Sam hugged Jesse back. "We got here a few hours ago. I got lost looking for your ma and then I ran into Savannah. You are right son. She is quite a stunning young woman."

Savannah tried to hide her surprise, even though her right eye had started to twitch. Then it began to jump and Savannah touched the corner of it, hoping to quell the twitching skin. Big Sam had known the whole time whom he was talking to which meant Jesse had brought her here to meet his family. She looked around the room for Mary Kate, trying to see if she was talking to his brother or mother. She didn't like surprises and thus far, he had heaped several upon her. The ring, the spa day with his sister, the afternoon coffee with his dad were all calculated moves on his part. The grin had left her face and Jesse almost felt the resentment that was shooting at him through Savannah's eyes.

Big Sam was the one to address Savannah in a low

tone, "Montgomery Construction is a family business. Our families work together and sometimes we play together, but most of all, we do business with other families. Every member is critical to the team's success." His hand caressed her arm. "Today and tomorrow are critical to getting contracts for the next year. You are a part of our team, Savannah."

He leaned in and kissed her cheek. "This is an important weekend for Jesse. He brought you here to be at his side to help him start something and build something new. Are you willing to lend him a hand, Savannah?"

Savannah softened the icy stare, adding a soft smirk aimed at Jesse. "In this dress, I am guaranteed to get you all the attention you need, Big Guy. Let's go make some deals." She linked her arm into Jesse's as they headed off to work the room, with Big Sam watching them closely. There was no denying the two made a stunning couple.

Mary Kate came to stand beside Big Sam. "Whatcha thinking about, Daddy?"

"Really pretty grandbabies," he muttered under his breath.

She had been played again, but she gave Jesse all smiles as he introduced her to his team. One gentleman even commented on her sweet potato pie, another on her apple pie, and one of the wives asked for her meatloaf recipe. He had told them all about her and shared what she had packed in his lunches. *Touching.*

There was so much pride in his eyes when he introduced her to his co-workers. Savannah thought about what he had said to her months ago, *I am cared for and loved, and I finally belong to someone. I am at peace.*

She was still pissed off, but now she understood. As she donned her warm trophy wife face, she cordially took the time to individually speak with every member of his team, their wives, and their girlfriends as if Jesse had told her about each and every one of them. At the end of the evening she was assimilated into the group and was accepted as a member of the team. Jesse said he finally belonged to someone and was at peace. Honestly, she was feeling the same.

Chapter Twenty-Five

It was 6:30 am Mountain Time when Savannah awoke. For the dumbest reason in the world, she attempted to hide her resentment of *meet my family* by going glass per glass with Big Sam. It was with a newfound respect that she realized that expensive wine or cheap wine had the same residual effects: a headache and an upset stomach. She had only had six glasses when Big Sam noticed her getting glassy-eyed. The first glass was consumed when he had snatched her away from Jesse and proceeded to parade her around the room like an affirmative action blue chip. The second and third glasses came when Mary Kate cornered her in the bathroom, suggesting her friends feel how firm and taut her butt cheeks were. Savannah stopped them all, gently explaining that it made her uncomfortable to be touched that way. Just to have fun, she added a sister girl neck roll, a lip smack, and put her hands on her hips in a defensive stance. The women loved it. *Great! Now I am going to be listed by each of them as their 'black friend.'*

The fourth glass magically appeared in her hand as Jesse whispered sweet nothings in her ear, telling her how fabulous she looked, and how he couldn't wait to get her back to the room. For the fifth glass, she had stepped behind the bar and poured it herself because she could not believe any of this shit. The sixth one was for good measure because Savannah liked even numbers.

She turned to her side and cracked open one eye to find Jesse lying there watching her. Nothing was said as he gazed at her with that quizzical look on his face, like a little monkey understanding if you pull the string, nuts will fall out of the hole in the wall. She knew that look. He had some random fucking question that he had been pondering for some time. May as well delve into the discussion. "Good morning to you as well," she said as she covered her sour wine saturated morning breath with her hand. "What is your burgeoning question of the day?"

Jesse blinked several times as he brushed a wayward lock of her hair from her face and then leaned in to kiss the tip of her nose. "We were a hit last night."

A hit of what? Insanity? She was drunker than Cooter Woods and had stood around looking like a deer in the headlights with a good dental plan. She was over all of it.

"What is the question, Jesse?"

He sensed the hostility that was still simmering under the surface, but he had been dealt this hand and he was going to play it. Systematically, step by step, he would move them toward a future, and some things needed to be discussed, so he asked, "Are you on birth control?"

Heavens to Betsy! "Is there a reason why we are discussing my reproductive choices before I have had my first cup of coffee?"

"I was just wondering. We have been seeing each other for nine months and I am still wearing condoms. I mean really, I have ingested enough of you at this point, that I feel like we are one."

Ingested? Well that was unexpected. Her real reason, although not scientifically documented because no one ever discussed such matters, was that mixing his DNA with hers would change her perfume. The quickest way for a man to know that a woman is cheating is by the smell. Adding another man's seed to an already tilled garden changes the taste of the fruit, thereby altering the chemistry of the nectar. She still managed to stay honest. "It is messy. I don't like messy."

"Love is messy, Savannah," he said as his fingers pushed away her hand so he could run the appendages across her lips. "I would like to get messy with you."

She wasn't in the mood. She smelled like sour wine, plus she was still angry about the Big Sam thing. "Well ..." she started, then changed her mind to pull one of his tactics. "... while we are on the subject of birth control, how soon do you think a couple should start planning a family after they marry?"

Without hesitation, he said, "Two years minimum, five years max." Her eyebrows arched. Jesse explained that a new couple needed time to understand how to live together, which takes about a year. The second year, the shine is off the new nickels and that time should be spent clarifying roles. Savannah questioned his word choice.

"Yes, roles. Understanding what is expected of me as your husband and what I would expect of you as my wife. Then we determine what your long term dream or goal is, as well as mine, and then we decide on our long term goals as a family." He smiled as he ran his thumb across her bottom lip.

Jesse kissed her lightly before he added, "You said you wanted at least three children, but you need at least a year in your new job role to make alliances, learn some tricks of the trade, and hold your position. At least a another year is needed to get really great at the business, so I figure we can begin our family at the start of our third year of marriage."

Suddenly, she wasn't so mad any more. She also found comfort in the way he spoke of them as one. "Savannah," he said as he pulled her closer to him. "I am out of condoms. I can get some more by tonight. If you wish to wait, I am okay with that...." He paused, waiting for her to say something. He didn't want to be crass and rub his throbbing body part against her, but he was about to lose his mind.

She asked, "And if I don't want to wait?"

He whispered in her ear, sending goose bumps down the right side of her entire body. "Then things are about to get really messy."

He knew her body well and she was ready within minutes to receive him. His movements were tentative and he pressed himself into her and froze. The look on his face was intense, as if he had inadvertently bumped his funny bone and the pain was just beginning to register in his brain and then on his face.

"Jesse, is something wrong?"

"It feels so magical, like I just stuck my dick in a fairy or something." His face was contorted like he was trying to process a complex algorithm.

Savannah only made it worse. "So, have you done that often, to a fairy, I mean?"

He moved slowly, still trying to find a distraction so he didn't embarrass himself like it was his first time. "Shhhh, I'm concentrating here, Tinkerbell, I don't want to make a premature mess." He frowned deeper as he was still having trouble focusing. "Savannah, damn, damn, damn," was all he said as he withdrew and thrust into her again and again.

Her fingers ran across his chest as she whispered

words of encouragement. Without the condom, she could feel the veins, the power, and the heat of him. Her hips matched his rhythm as she thrust upward to meet his movements. It felt so good; she rolled upward on her back to the higher part of her shoulders, throwing a leg over his right shoulder while using her left foot for leverage on his hip. She rolled her hip down, then upward and his eyes grew wide. He brought her left leg up on his shoulder, forcing her name out through gritted teeth as he pumped everything he had into her when he felt the start of her climax. He yelled out her name as it tingled all the way to his toes, every nerve in his body lit, humming, singing her praises.

Jesse was winded, breathing hard, mumbling while still entangled with her as he reached for the nightstand to get his phone.

"Jesse, who are you calling at this hour?"

"My bank," he said as he scrolled through the numbers.

Savannah didn't understand how after making such passionate love, he needed to make a phone call, let alone to his bank. "No one is open at this time of morning. Can't it wait until we've had our breakfast, showered, and prepared for our day?"

He kissed her again and was shaking his head profusely. "Nope, I got to start the paperwork, sell some stock, some blood or something...."

Now, she was getting irritated with him. "Jesse! What are you talking about?"

"Shit, that was so good, I need to call some dammed body. Plus, you said you wanted a C-Class, Sapphire Gray Metallic, four doors. Fuck it! I think I am going to buy you two!"

She laughed as she took the phone from his hands. "Funny, really funny," she told him as she rolled him to his back and perched herself on top of him. "How about I call and order us some breakfast instead."

"Order whatever you want, as long as I can have a second helping of you." His hands slid under her pajama top. A big laugh escaped her throat when at the most inappropriate time she thought of her brother. She was about to partake in some full-fledged dick riding and today, she felt like covering Jesse in some serious fairy dust.

Things were about to get really messy. Especially considering she was really liking the idea of being his wife.

Chapter Twenty-Six

Jesse was brief in his explanation of her itinerary for the day, as it had changed since last night. She would spend the morning with driving lessons with his brother Joe and then have lunch with his mother, who had not made an appearance last night. The first thing Savannah commented on was his mother's name, which was Ruth, who was married to Samuel. "Are you kidding me? You guys are Jesse, Mary and Joseph?"

"We are Southern Baptist," he said as he shrugged and headed for the door after kissing her cheek.

Savannah's head was still spinning. This was all going horribly wrong, but felt so damned good, so she decided to enjoy it versus ruining her first romantic getaway. Technically, it was a work conference for him, but she had been treated to the spa, was about to receive driving lessons, and have a late lunch with a man's mother that she actually liked and respected. She was really looking forward to meeting the rest of Jesse's family.

In rectitude she should be running, but his family was so accepting, not condescending, nor making her feel like she was a second-class citizen. She dressed in a hurry and headed downstairs. She wore a pair of loose-fitting black slacks along with a long-sleeved lavender polo with the Montgomery Construction logo on it that Jesse had brought her. When she rounded the corner, she immediately spotted Joe, who also had piercing blue eyes, and brownish colored hair, unlike Jesse and Mary Kate, who both had black hair. He was a cross between Big Sam and Mary Kate. She figured he must look like Ruth. "Hi

Joe," she said as she walked up and extended her hand. "I am Savannah. Nice to meet you."

He accepted her shake and led her out the door. He was far more reserved and less cordial than Big Sam. She held her judgment of him, as he was doing of her, until they had a feel of each other. No words were exchanged as they ambled along in the golf cart and arrived at the driving range. "Jess said you had never golfed before, so I am going to teach you some basic driving techniques." She nodded and listened to everything he said, focusing mainly on grip and setting up the ball, the swing position, and the finishing position.

Savannah watched Joe closely, asking him to repeat the movement at least three times.

He stared at her.

She stared at him.

She took the club, speaking out loud his steps as she positioned herself over the ball.

Joe corrected her verbally and then moved in closer to touch her. Savannah jumped like a cat in a room full of red laser lights. Joe held up his hands. "Sorry, didn't mean to invade your space."

Savannah had nothing to lose. "After yesterday with your sister, I am just a bit more cautious."

"Oh, she felt you up, huh?"

Savannah looked at him with genuine surprise registered on her mug. *Did they discuss such things?*

"Did Mary Kate tell you she was gay?"

The club hung loosely in her hand as her mouth draped open. Joe broke into laughter. "Nawww, she isn't, I was just messing with you."

She playfully hit him with the club. "Not funny, Joe,

especially since you knew it had crossed my mind. So how did you know?"

"She has a thing for boobs. She is obsessed and wants to have the surgery, but she's scared. So she feels up every nice pair she sees, testing which ones are real and which are enhanced by saline." He admitted that she had done the same to his last girlfriend, as well as the current one, who now refused to be alone with Mary Kate.

After a few cordial platitudes, Savannah told him "Okay, If I hit this ball a few times, can we head back to the hotel and order a couple of glasses of something alcoholic before I meet your mother?"

"Only if you get it right, if not, I am going to torture you until you do," he said it so matter-of-factly that Savannah accepted his challenge.

She approached the tee and pinched her thumb and forefinger in a pattern that formed a V pointed toward her right shoulder. She overlapped her left hand on the grip and bent forward on her hips, standing shoulder width apart. A perfect triangle was formed as she brought her swing back so that the butt of the driver was aimed at the ball. Her hips began to turn as she brought the club into her downswing, making contact with the ball and sending it flying down the modified fairway. It was textbook perfect.

Joe's mouth was open. "No fricking way. I'll bet you can't do that again!"

Savannah took her position, repeated the steps, and once again sent the ball flying down the fairway. Before Joe could open his mouth, she repeated it again, then again, and once more for good measure. She removed the glove and took a seat in the golf cart. "It's simple mathematics Now enough of this shit. This is as close to a vacation as I am going to get for a while, so let's get out of here, Joe."

Joe bent his six-foot frame over and began to laugh. "You are something else." The ride back had a totally different vibe as he talked about himself and his role at Montgomery Construction. It did not take Joe long to understand that his big brother's girlfriend had no inkling what Jesse did for a living.

Joe explained that there were two divisions in the company, residential and commercial, with Jesse working the residential multi-unit side. The conference was an opportunity to broker new contracts and deals. The first few days, he told her, were all continuing education classes and product demonstrations. The last few days were family connection days. "I hate to believe such nepotism still exists in the business world, but in this business, it does. You do business with me, you do business with my family."

Savannah asked few questions, which perplexed Joe. "Aren't you interested in what he does?"

"Not really, because at the end of the day, he leads a team that builds stuff," she said as the golf cart pulled up to the main entrance of the hotel. "When he steps through the front door, my job is to make him forget the office, decompress, and fortify him to return the next day. It makes little sense for him to bring the office into *our* home." She extended her hand. "Nice to meet you, Joe."

At the doorway, she bumped into the ladies who were with Mary Kate last night, and they convinced her to join some of the other family members for board games in one of the conference rooms. Joe was intrigued and followed along. Once Savannah saw the chessboard, she took a seat, followed by Joe. Two hours had passed and she had beaten him three times. She looked at her watch. "Oh! Gotta run and freshen up before I meet your Mom for lunch."

She patted Joe on the shoulder. "Bishop to King Three and checkmate."

Joe watched her walk away.

Jesse was coming through the double doors. Savannah stopped and shared a few words with him, as Joe watched her caress his brother's arm, then place her hand over his heart, whisper in his ear, and disappear. Joe was still staring.

"So, how'd it go, Joe?" Jesse asked his younger brother by three years who served as the director of contracts for Montgomery Construction.

"Where in the world did you find her?" he asked Jesse, still staring at the door.

Jesse was concerned. "Why? Is something wrong?"

"No," he said as he turned back around to see Jesse resetting the chessboard. "I just need you to go back and get another one for me."

The two brothers laughed and enjoyed a few turns at the chessboard. It had been Jesse's only break since arriving at the conference.

Chapter Twenty-Seven

Savannah entered the hotel restaurant and quickly spotted a woman whom she thought could be Jesse's mother. To her embarrassment, the lady was not and looked at her as if she had grown an extra eye. As she turned, she spotted a matronly woman surrounded by a group of young girls, who looked up and winked at her. Ruth was a very attractive woman who dripped Southern gentility in her every word and move. She wore a Montgomery Construction pink silk blouse, a black skirt with pink trim, and black shoes on a kitten heel. There was no doubt in Savannah's mind that the Wilma Flintstone-sized pearls around her neck were real and amazingly so was the smile she gave to Savannah.

Extending her hand for a shake, Ruth smacked it lightly and opted to embrace Savannah. Her voice was laced with a deep Southern accent that was reminiscent of Scarlet O'Hara. "It is such a pleasure to meet you, Savannah," she said. As Ruth held her at arm's length, taking in every nuance of Savannah's physical being as if to make a mental photograph of her features.

Just as quickly as the love fest started, it ended when Ruth exclaimed, "Oh cement in a bucket!" Not quite sure what that meant, Savannah's eyes grew wide as she followed the line of sight to what Ruth was staring at. There were two ladies about Ruth's age barreling down on them.

Ruth told Savannah, "Follow my lead. These two are the biggest gossips east and west of the Mississippi. I can barely stomach either of them...." Her voice trailed off as she faced the ladies with cordial grace. "Eudora, Katy Mae." She grinned while greeting them as they exchanged air kisses, impersonating affection.

Eudora sported a Baxter Construction shirt and Katy Mae wore a Waldorf Builders shirt-dress that did absolutely nothing for her figure. The figure, if one could call it that, was more obelisk in shape, leading up to a thin neck supporting a very large head. It took everything Savannah had not to stare at the woman, who had a horse-like face.

Eudora was the first to speak. "Ruth, darling, who is this charming creature?" All eyes were now on Savannah. She looked to Ruth, who took the lead. "This is Dr. Savannah Niden."

Emily piped up, "Is she a new addition to the Montgomery Construction family?"

It was sad how much Ruth was enjoying this. Savannah watched with amusement as Jesse's mom began the game of cat and mouse with the two women, feeding them just enough cheese to lure them into her trap. "In more ways than one, girls."

Eudora's eyes were wide as she looked at Savannah's left hand, spying the ring and grabbing her fingers, holding the hand in the middle of the group. "Don't tell me Joe has finally settled down and decided to stop breaking hearts."

The look on Ruth's face was worth the airfare. It was executed with perfection and Savannah was thoroughly impressed. "Joe ..." Ruth exhaled. "That young man goes through women like a bag of Lay's. I swear he can't snack on just one." She paused, allowing the words to hover in the air before spreading the last bit on rather thickly, "Savannah belongs to my Jesse."

If she had not been standing so close to Eudora and Katy Mae, she would have sworn they had stopped breathing. This was fun. Savannah wanted in. "Mom, I think you might be right. Looking at this gem from this angle, the wedding ring should just be a gold band with no diamonds."

Ruth concurred. She looped her arm through Savannah's and pulled her hand away from the bug-eyed women. They excused themselves and followed a waiter to their table. Savannah looked over her shoulder adding, "It was a pleasure meeting you both."

Savannah was uncertain if using *'Mom'* had been appropriate and she was pleased when they reached their table in *The Tavern* and Ruth said, "The Mom bit was a nice touch. Now let me see that ring."

Ruth special ordered a Niçoise salad and recommended it for Savannah as well, who declined. "That much oil, fish, and garlic in one meal makes you smell like a bad night in the red light district." She immediately bit her lip. Ruth pondered her words then changed her order to a beefsteak tomato Caprese while Savannah opted for the Phillips salad on Belgian endive. Since her salad did not have meat, she also ordered *tarte flambee* flatbread with bacon and Gruyère cheese.

"Ruth, I hope you don't mind me asking, but if those two are the biggest gossips, why did we give them so much fodder?"

Sipping on her ice tea, Ruth said, "Well, if people are going to gossip, I say give them something good to blather about."

"The ring was just a gift and it is a topaz, not a chocolate diamond. It doesn't mean what we implied."

"It implied enough to keep Eudora from trying to fob that horse-faced daughter of hers off on us or Jesse."

Savannah wasn't buying it and Ruth surmised as much. "This is a cutthroat business. You either move with the times or get rolled over. You are a breath of fresh air to these stale proceedings and I am glad you are here."

She sipped at her water, looking at the clear blue eyes that Jesse inherited from his mother. "I just don't want to upset Jesse when it gets back to him."

Ruth threw back her perfectly coiffed gray-haired head and let out the most unladylike guffaw. "Dear, you are the first woman he has ever brought to any conference and he has been attending them for the past twenty something years. That, in itself, speaks for him."

There was nothing more for Savannah to say, so she enjoyed her lunch. Much of the conversation focused on personal interest as the two women spoke of hobbies and career choices. Ruth took a minute to go over some facts about Jesse that Savannah did not know. The one that made her arch her brow was when Ruth told her, "Jesse has an IQ of 170 and loves to build things. He is great with his hands, which works well for the family while harnessing his energy. That man has more energy than a bunny on speed."

"He does have a lot energy. It even amazes me sometimes," she said. Her mind went to this morning, thinking of her lover going at it like a rabbit in heat. It was difficult to stay focused as Savannah agreed that the man was wonderful with his hands and she loved his energy levels.

Savannah remembered trying to explain some of the bigger words she had used, thinking he didn't understand when his IQ was higher than hers. She tuned back in to hear Ruth comment, "Just think, Big Sam and I will have beautiful genius grandbabies." Savannah almost choked.

Ruth went on to order tea as if what she'd said had no more bearing than telling those women that "Savannah belongs to my Jesse."

All in all, it was a great lunch. Savannah took care of the tab with some of the funds she had left over from Jesse's check then headed back to her room for some R & R. She was asleep in less than 30 minutes.

Jesse arrived at the room at 3:30 to find Savannah sprawled out on the bed, sleeping peacefully. The woman had such a beautiful spirit. He tried not to wake her as he slipped into the bed. She turned on her right side in a fetal position. He draped his arms over her waist and his hand came in contact with the ring. Idly, his fingers toyed with his gift. It was the perfect colored chocolate diamond for the woman he was determined to make his wife. The words that accompanied the present had been lost in the confusion on her face over breakfast yesterday. He had wanted to ask her to marry him. It took him several days before her arrival to find the right combination of words. As she slept, he whispered the words he had chosen into the back of her hair.

"Choose me as your husband, Tinkerbell, and give this lost boy a home."

The instant Jesse's weight sank onto the bed, Savannah came awake. She heard his words and understood what he wanted. What bugged her most was she was uncertain if she possessed the wherewithal to give it, not only to him, but also to Darwin. Her heart had been closed off for so many years that loving Jesse as she did elicited a bevy of unresolved issues yet to be addressed.

Tinkerbell was the one who was lost.

Chapter Twenty-Eight

The black tie affair was truly a grand spectacle. All of the men were in black tuxedos and the women wore black evening gowns. It was dinner and dancing and no one was on the podium pontificating about construction. It was an opportunity to dress up, trip the light fantastic, and get really fancy. Savannah loved it.

Jesse looked flawless in his tux and the whole family cleaned up rather nicely. Joe and his girlfriend, Alana, looked magnificent as they posed for pictures in front of the makeshift photo studio. The photographer and his assistant had a sweet set- up which printed pictures on site. She and Jesse took a few shots together. Savannah refused to even think about where and if she would ever be able to display them.

Savannah made her way to the bar to once more hide in her glass of wine but was approached by a tall dark-skinned African American gentleman as well as a fairer, younger version of himself. Cordial was her middle name; she acknowledged both men and addressed the bartender for a glass of Chenin Blanc. The younger of two gentlemen moved in closer and uttered something revolting to her, then had the audacity to actually reach out to touch her. "Put your hand back in your pocket and take two steps back," she said as quietly as he had spoken to her so no one else could hear them. "I am uncertain of which manhole you chewed your way through, but you will not denigrate or disparage me with your tawdry retorts. It is not that type of party."

Instead of him acquiescing and politely walking away, he played the race card. "Oh so it's like that! A brother can't get no play once you start hanging out with the duck dynasty!"

Although he raised his voice, she refused to do the same. "Maybe you can't get any play, *my brother*, because you don't have any game."

He almost spat the word *bitch* and walked away. That did it! She had the bartender refill her glass only to turn and find the older gentleman still standing there. "I'm sorry. Men here tend to be overly friendly to a point of discomfort. So many connections are made and any woman that is unattached, or assumed to be, and men go nuts."

He apologized for the younger man and started up a conversation with her. He had warm eyes and a nice smile that made Savannah feel comfortable, and he asked her to call him Bob. *He knew who she was, as did the other man. What was this, a test?*

"Dr. Niden?" he asked in a lowered tone. "If you were to describe Jesse in one word, what word would you use?"

It did not take Savannah long to decide when she said, "Detailed." She looked at him with all sincerity. "He is one of those rare men who can see the whole picture, understand the process of making it all come together, and possesses the skill set to make it happen." She cocked her head to the right. "That's what sets him apart, his attention to the details." She looked down at the beautiful birthstone ring. She wasn't even aware that she had mentioned her birthday was in November, but if she had, he remembered. "The devil is always in the details."

The answer must have satisfied Bob, who asked her if

he could have the honor of a dance later in the evening. Savannah patted his hand and returned the wine glass to the bartender. "Later is word used by people with poor planning skills," she said as she pulled him by the arm to the dance floor. He held her as a father would a daughter and they maneuvered effortlessly across the dance floor.

Her dancing did not stop there as she did a two-step with Big Sam, joined in on *The Wobble* with Mary Kate, and worked profusely to not lose her rhythm as Joe gyrated on the floor like he was having an epileptic fit. The final dance of the evening was a couple's dance.

Jesse rose slowly from the table and asked for her hand, leading her out on the floor, and pulled her in close. "I am not much of a dancer, Savannah, but I welcome any opportunity to hold you close." One hand rested in the small of her back, their interlocked hands held over his heart. He smelled fantastic and looked even better. She loved this man. *Dear Lord in Heaven, I am also in love with this man.*

"I saw you dancing with Bob Walker," he whispered in her ear.

"And ... I also spent three hours with Big Sam and had no clue who he was either. This is your world. I am just trying to make a good impression for you."

He stopped moving and looked down at her. "I am impressed each time you look at me or confess your love for me. Nothing and nobody else matters." The music had also stopped but all eyes were on them as Jesse lowered his head and captured her mouth with his own. There were wolf whistles and hoots all around them, as her Tool Man created another magical moment that would factor into an upcoming choice that would soon need to be made.

Thus far, Savannah was thoroughly enjoying the trip. She had some downtime to relax and today was the final event, the pool party. It baffled her somewhat that the organization would sponsor a pool party in October in Colorado Springs. The zero entry infinity pool was a magnificent sight to see as the back edge of it jutted up against Cheyenne Lake, and she used her cell phone to snap pictures.

Savannah wore a red cover-up over her one-piece suit and moderate heels as she made her way poolside. Her eyes were wide, as the construction companies had transformed the pool area with four massive grills, an outdoor dance floor, and a buffet that would make anyone's mouth water. Even though it was 70 degrees, some of the adults ventured into the water. Jesse explained that the pool party was more symbolic than practical. "It started when I was a kid. We went to Vegas or Lake Havasu or somewhere in the summer and the last day of the conference was always a pool party." He grimaced as he thought of the poor planning for this one. Each year, instead of continuing education courses and fellowship with fellow construction families, these meetings were bombarded with sales people. People who sold everything from bulldozers to lunch boxes. The organizers wanted to make sure the heavy equipment operators were unable to get much of the product up the mountain, shifting the focus of the conference to business deals and classes. "It was good training this year."

Later in the evening as they packed in their room, he showed her the certificates he had earned, as well as new

CPR certification, and some other things she did not understand. He was proud as he shared each piece of paper with her. She fussed and fawned over each sheet he showed her, proud of what each sheet represented for him. Even prouder that he had chosen to share his world with her.

"I'll get you some frames for these." She didn't know if he had an office, but either way, next week she would have six new frames to place each certificate in.

There was also a stack of new business contacts that he seemed truly excited about. "Next year is going to be my best year ever, Savannah!" He picked her up in his arms and twirled her about the room.

"Thank you for coming and being here with me. It has meant a lot."

"It has meant a lot to me as well, Jesse. Thank you for inviting me."

In front of the ridiculously warm fireplace, he made love to her slowly, not wanting the evening the end. "I can't seem to get enough you, my lovely ... never enough."

Chapter Twenty-Nine

November

Little was said again about the trip as Savannah arrived home that Sunday afternoon and began to plan for her week. Darwin asked few questions and she offered few details of her getaway. His only comment was, "You seem so relaxed."

Savannah chalked it up to the spa. They chatted a bit more about her birthday gathering the following week as well as dinner with his parents on Saturday night. As the week swung by, she seemed to be in another world. The cramps from her monthly made her poor company on Thursday night when Jesse came over. He placed an electric heating pad to her abdomen, which made her sweaty but relieved some of the pain. During the night, he held her close and rubbed her stomach as if he was willing away the discomfort. She told him next Thursday was off since she had to prep the house for Friday night.

Time was running out for them and soon Savannah would have to choose. It was a precarious position Jesse found himself in. He knew that it wasn't just two hours that could have changed their lives, but it was also the reasoning of a woman. For now, this was all he had and he hoped that what he had done thus far would be enough for her to choose him. There was one final play he had to make, and he would do that next week.

Savannah was excited about her birthday and turning 30. Finally, feeling as if she had grown into her womanhood. Her confidence level was up. She felt sexy, alive, and ready to conquer the world. This was going to be a fun evening with family and friends and she was a little saddened that she had been a chicken shit and had not invited Jesse. *Now, if he had only taken the hint.*

Jerwane never believed it was too cold or too hot to barbeque. Traci was making margaritas, Sheryl was amusing a few of her co-workers, and Savannah's mom stood in the corner chatting with Darwin. Cassiopeia had arrived with a gift, overdressed, over-made, and looking like she stepped out of a bad episode of *Real Housewives from Hell*. Savannah thanked her and poured her a glass of wine. A few neighbors popped in, along with a college buddy and a few other faces. Carolina, her coworker, came with her husband and daughter, Nayla. There were a few other small children there as well. Savannah saw no need to tell the parents not to invite the kids. She stepped outside for a moment to check the meat on the grill and got wrapped up in a conversation with Jerwane and his girlfriend, Donna.

Jesse quietly arrived and was greeted immediately by Darwin, who then introduced him to Savannah's mother, who was in the kitchen making barbecue sauce. "It is a pleasure to meet you Mrs. Niden, I'm Jesse."

Nothing escaped Emurial's attention. She knew her daughter's affinity for an ordered life and she knew her schedule. It was easy to deduce who this man was. "Ah, Thursdays."

Jesse's eyes were wide. *Had Savannah told her mother about me?*

"You have some nerve coming here, young man," she said with full admonishment in a hushed tone.

"She is my friend and it is her birthday, but I didn't come to see her, I came to meet you." He had Emurial's full attention.

She wasn't fazed by his tactics. "And why would you need to do that?"

He turned his body at an angle and lowered his voice, "I wanted to know how her beauty would gracefully age, as well as being curious about your feelings on cream-colored grandbabies."

Emurial didn't blink, but instead she seemed to grow another two inches when she found her answer. "The skin tone of the children doesn't matter. What matters is what kind of husband and father you would be."

As if the Heavens had heard her words, Jesse felt a tug at his pants leg and looked down to see the cutest two-year-old that had ever graced the planet. She was covered in a fine sheen of cocoa, with large brown eyes and two rather large afro- puffs which seemed to double the size of her little head. She held out her hands to Jesse, saying the words, "Up pweeease."

Jesse looked at Emurial, who said with some authority, "Well, pick her up." As if he had found the map to the treasure of the Sierra Madre, he lifted the child slowly and held her at arm's length, looking at Emurial for guidance. With a shake of her head, she gripped Jesse's arms and showed him how to hold the child.

The little girl, Nayla, did not make it easy after she heard the ticking of his watch when he patted one of the little afro-puffs. She giggled as she pressed her ear to his wrist listening to the ticking. "Down, pwease." Jesse lowered her to the floor and she scampered off. He shrugged his shoulders, ready to continue his conversation with Savannah's mother but was halted by another tug on his pants leg. This time when he looked down, the little one had collected every child at the party. Each child wanted to hear his watch and Jesse squatted, patiently giving each child a turn.

Nayla had disappeared and returned to the kitchen with *A Little Golden Book.* She shoved it in Jesse's face. "Story pweeease." He was still looking at Emurial for help, who pushed him toward the couch and helped him get comfortable. He took a seat and Nayla climbed into his lap. On his left side was a little boy who seemed only mildly interested, while the other four children sat at his feet.

Jesse looked at his new audience. "Are we ready for an adventure, guys?" The little heads bobbed up and down. He read the title of the book and opened the cover. Jesse read the story to Nayla's little crew, using voices and an animated face, which made the children crack up with laughter, as if what he was saying was the funniest thing in the world. With each section he read, he would turn and show the illustrations to the kids. The room got quiet while he read each page, and even the parents came into the room to listen, while he held the children's attention.

Savannah noticed the quietness and walked into the dining area and was shocked to see Jesse sitting there in the midst of all the children, looking as comfortable as the day was long. It took everything in Savannah not to beam with pride, but instead she walked over and stood beside her mother, who kept all expression from her face, a skill that her mother had also taught her.

As Jesse read the last page, he lowered the tone in his voice so the children would know the story was ending. He closed the book and the kids clapped along some of the parents, and he seemed shocked by all the attention as he looked up to see Savannah standing there.

Rising slowly, he walked over to Savannah with Nayla perched on his hip, holding her as Emurial had shown him. He seldom if ever held his little cousin because he was afraid he would break her, so holding this child was a new experience for him. He liked holding her and immediately thought of the day in their future when it would be little Sahara on his hip and he would be reading her stories.

"Hi, Jesse," Savannah said casually, as she shook his hand. "I wasn't expecting you." He smiled coolly as he handed her the box that pulled from his cargo pocket. "Happy Birthday."

Darwin displayed little couth as he asked loudly, "What is that?"

Jesse looked at Savannah, who stated, "I'm with Darwin. It is an oddly shaped box. What is it?"

"A Dozuki dovetail saw," Jesse said and Savannah's eyes lit up. She threw herself at him and hugged him tightly and even planted a small kiss on his jaw. Emurial Niden did not let it go unnoticed. Jesse's hand went in the air, not touching her as he stepped back, still holding the child. "Okay, okay, are you trying to get me shot by your fiancé?"

Everyone laughed it off, but Emurial and Jerwane, who had walked back in as they heard the commotion stood frozen in the doorway as Darwin and Jesse stood next to each other. Jerwane thought that either Jesse had the largest set he had ever seen on a man, or his sister did.

Once the commotion died down, Jesse found another opportunity to speak with Emurial alone while Savannah went back to her guests. Nayla was handed back to her mother so the conversation could be continued, "As I was saying earlier, Mrs. Niden, I wanted to meet you."

"I don't understand why it is important," she told him calmly, aware that every other eye in the room was upon her and her daughter's *friend*.

"I am planning to be a permanent fixture," he said with confidence.

Emurial didn't like the implication. "What about your family? Are they okay with your plans?"

"My family wants me to be happy. She makes me happy. And besides," he told her as she gave him a spoon to sample her sauce. "They love Savannah."

Emurial nearly dropped the large spoon she was using to stir the pot, asking Jesse, "And when did your family meet my daughter?" she asked through clipped tones with her back turned to the crowd.

Jesse followed her lead, "Last month in Colorado Springs." He smiled at her, saying aloud as he tasted the sauce, "That is good stuff. Does Savannah have this recipe?"

Darwin stood back, watching as all eyes in the room focused on Jesse chatting amicably with Emurial. Jerwane stood beside him. "Do you ever feel like some days you are just losing the race, Darwin?"

He looked at Jerwane with his lip turned up. "No. I don't lose. Your sister is marrying me."

Savannah tried hard to not show any outward feelings about Jesse being here, but Emurial noticed it in her eyes. "You are going to have to choose."

"What are you talking about, Mother?"

Emurial pinched her arm. "When I turn my back, I want you to look across the room at your fiancé."

Savannah turned and recoiled at the look on Darwin's face. There was hatred in his eyes as every eye in the room focused on Jesse. She was about to go to his side when she heard applause. In her appreciation, Nayla grabbed Jesse by the face and planted a very wet raspberry on his cheek. He thanked the little darling for the special fairy kiss and asked to borrow her book for one second.

Approaching Savannah and Emurial, his eyes were narrow and his massive paw nearly covered the front of the book, "I will take this as my cue to leave."

Neither lady argued, but Jesse was not finished. "If that was not a sign, then maybe this will be." He handed the book to Savannah, waved goodbye, and exited the front door. Savannah looked down at the book and her breath caught. It was *Tinkerbell*.

Darwin took it upon himself to walk Jesse out, while Jesse made sure he stayed out of Darwin's striking range. As they entered the stairwell, Jesse stood on the bottom landing while Darwin remained several steps above him.

"I had been meaning to thank you for putting in a word for me at Montgomery Construction. I got the position, but you know that already."

Jesse was not going to admit anything to that man, but he knew where the conversation was headed. "I got you the interview, you did the rest."

Darwin became defensive. "Oh is that what you tell yourself so you can sleep at night, that you helped me get the interview?"

With his arms at his side and his fists clenched, Jesse continued, "You sat at the table, over a meatloaf dinner that you barely touched and explained what you wanted, even going so far to lay out the impact it would have on your relationship. Yet, you made the choice to pursue the job, especially after you saw my shirt."

"So that makes what you are doing okay?"

"I am not sure what it is you think I'm doing, Darwin. You wanted your shot in the big field. You asked, and I opened the door."

Darwin didn't like to lose. "At the end of the day, Jesse, she is wearing my ring."

"If you check her other hand, you will notice she is also wearing mine."

He took a step toward Jesse, who did not move. "At the end of the day, Darwin, the choice is ultimately hers, but ..." he paused. "... I am a gentleman and I will make you a gentleman's agreement."

"Make your offer," Darwin said through tight lips.

"I will step out of the picture after the holidays." He extended his hand to Darwin to shake on it. When Darwin slipped his hand into Jesse's, he clamped down on the grip and yanked Darwin in close, almost crushing his hand. "Once she decides, the other man walks away, no muss, no fuss. Business will continue as normal."

Jesse's blue eyes pierced into Darwin's brown ones, with Darwin asking Jesse, "So you are saying that when she stays with the man she made the commitment to, you are not going to get me fired?"

"No. I am telling you that when she chooses me, to not be a bitch about it."

He released his hand and backed away, slowly going down the stairs to his truck.

Darwin knew he was on borrowed time. He liked that idea even less than he liked Jesse. Knowing he respected the man and what he did, only intensified his anger. Jesse Orison was really good at this job and had, on the few interactions Darwin had with him on the job, taught him several things. He was also the man who had taught his sweet Savannah to be nasty in bed.

That, he could not respect.

Chapter Thirty

<u>December</u>

Savannah was experiencing difficulty breathing. She sat straight up in the bed and found herself gasping for air. *What day was it? Where am I?* She reached out for Jesse, but he wasn't there. She reached for the other side of the bed for Darwin, but he wasn't there. Clouds poured into the ceiling and darkened the room, instilling trepidation and fear in her heart. She could hear her mother's voice warning her again. "You have got to choose, Baby. You can't keep playing with these men's emotions." Tossing and turning she tried to pull away. She heard footsteps as she ran blindly into the raindrops that were dropping horizontally to her chest.

The drowning feeling wasn't going away. The water was coming up over her head and her breathing was becoming laborious. She tried screaming for help, but no words came out. This was it. *Savannah Niden, you are dying.* Her last breaths were coming. She didn't know whom she wanted to leave her last words to. "I love you so much," she whispered as she began to surrender to the darkness.

Jesse sat up in the bed and caressed her face. "Savannah. Wake up, Sweetheart, wake up, Baby." He nudged her gently.

She awoke with a start. He pulled her into his arms and held her close until she stopped trembling. "Jesse, I can't go on like this. It's killing me. I'm not sleeping, I'm barely eating, and the nightmares are getting worse."

"The nightmares are driven by fear, Savannah. What are you afraid of losing?"

"You," she said as tears began to fall from her eyes. "I don't want to lose you." There were a myriad of words, phrases, and logical statements he could interject into this scenario extolling his virtues and why she should choose him over Darwin, but he wouldn't play into it. If she wanted him, he was here. If not, he would tuck his tail between his legs and move on.

Tonight he would just hold her and fantasize a few more times that he had come home from work to his beautiful wife.

It was one week until Christmas and Savannah looked like hell. Darwin was nice enough to point it out to her over dinner with his mother. Mrs. Finney expressed genuine concern. "You may need to see your physician, dear. Is the new position too much for you?"

It was the hatred she had seen in Darwin's eyes that had her worried. It was making her sick and she knew something had to be done. Emurial refused to discuss any of it with her. "I raised you better than to do what you are doing, girl."

"Mother, I love them both in very different ways," she tried to explain.

"Sweetheart, which one will make a good husband and father? More importantly, which one makes you the happiest?"

It was about more than just feeling happy. It was about building a life with a man who would not run off and leave her to raise two small children, a man who would not die at 42 and leave her in a ton of debt, as her father had done with them.

"It's time for you to have a conversation with them both."

Savannah agreed. She would start with Jesse.

Chapter Thirty - One

Jesse arrived at the house two days before Christmas carrying a box with holes in it. "Don't shake it or drop it, please," Jesse told her as Savannah took the box and sat down on the couch. Slowly, she lifted the lid to reveal a beautiful all white Birman kitten. Savannah immediately fell in love with the little beauty.

"What should I name her?" she asked Jesse.

He smiled at her. "How about Thursday?"

The pretty kitten immediately took to Savannah, who planted kisses on her head. Jesse took a seat next to her. "You have to choose, Savannah. I have a busy year ahead of me and I want you at my side. I want to come home to you every day, not just on Thursday."

She looked at him with tears in her eyes. He could see the fear. He needed to know what was she so afraid of, why he could not get her to say yes. The question was asked and she answered, "It's the children, Jesse, and being hungry." She explained that her childhood had been horrible. She looked different than the other kids, had a different grade of hair, and that made her a target.

"I was fifteen before I felt like I belonged anywhere. I don't want that for my children. I want them to fit in."

"That is dumbest thing I have ever heard! Our children will have confidence in who they are because we will show them. We will teach them understanding and tolerance. Our children will be magnificent. They will be smart, wise, considerate, and charitable because that is who we are, and they shall learn from us. They will know both sides of their heritage because our families will share in their upbringing."

Her tears were more than he could handle. "I love you, Savannah. I am asking you to choose me. Choose me because you love me and you want to build a life together. Pick me because you want to go to bed at night beside me and wake up to me for the rest your life."

"Jesse, you don't understand what it is like to struggle for every dime and meal and have the money to keep the lights on."

"I understand that as man and wife, there may be times when we will have peanut butter sandwiches for dinner because it is all we have. I understand that in winter we may have to burn the wood fireplace so we can make the payment on the house and your fancy car. I understand that we may have to forgo a cruise one year because little Sahara will need braces or Daniel's athletic dues will put us in a pinch, but as man and wife, we climb those mountains together. We do what we have to do to move forward."

She said nothing for a few seconds. "My father died and left us in a world of debt that my mother had no clue he had. My sixteen-year-old brother became a man and took on a full time job while in school to help pay the bills. I have been hungry more times than I care to imagine. I am trying to be fair, but I must look out for my future and my aging mother."

Jesse jumped up from the couch. "Don't you dare talk to me about fair, Savannah!" Her eyes grew wide in disbelief as his face turned red with anger.

"You invited me inside! You pulled this lost boy into

your tree house of treasures. You fed me, nurtured me, cared for me, and loved me like I have never been loved. You cooked me breakfast before packing my lunch and fortifying me for another week. Now you want to chop off my hand and feed it to a croc and tell me I can't have any of this? That is unfair, Savannah! You are unfair, and you are the bad guy!" Jesse placed one hand on his hip, rolled his neck, and pointed a finger at her.

Savannah was trying to process everything he had said, but what bothered her was his delivery. "Did you just sister girl me?"

Jesse's eyes got wide and he rolled his neck again, smacking his lips. Savannah found his reaction more disturbing than his constant references to the JM Barrie story.

"You do realize in that story that those kids are dead, and Peter is the angel leading them to heaven, right, which is why the boys never aged?"

"I know that, Savannah, and it is how I feel with you. I want it all. What you are asking for in return is nothing. You want the house? Fine, you can have the house if I have to build it my gosh damned myself. I will work side projects to get you the car, if those are your main concerns, but those are not the factors that make up a good marriage. And anyone that convinces you otherwise is lying to you. I don't want a trophy wife or some dullard who spends her days shopping and watching TV. I want a wife that loves me, someone I can talk to, share ideas and build something with. I want a helpmate in a woman that I can love back."

Savannah had nothing more to say on the matter right now. She wanted time to think about what she needed to decide.

He helped her with her decision. "I will step out of the picture. You have until the end of January. On February 1st, I will move on if I have not heard from you."

He planted a kiss on her forehead. "Have a Merry Christmas." He walked to the door, and looking back at her with somber eyes before he reminded her, "You have the number."

Jesse sat in the room with his parents, watching nothing in particular as his folks opened their presents. Savannah had given him a box that he hadn't bothered to open when he was with her. Emotions consumed him like a pit of black ooze clambering up his leg, overtaking his breathing, and it was taking a concerted effort to maintain some calmness in front of his parents. He opened the box to remove two new fishing poles, a pair of moisturizing socks, some new cologne, and a shirt in the funny blue color she liked. *What if she doesn't choose me?*

It was his first moment of doubt. Tired fingers rubbed his eyes as he conceptually tried to put together a plan to move on if he wasn't going to be her husband. There was no room in his mind to be her boyfriend, her lover, or a continuation of Thursday nights. If she agreed and picked him, he would marry her the next week. Darwin, the dumbass, had waited a year and look where it got him. His thoughts went back to the guy in the parking garage, salivating and choking on his own saliva while holding onto his nuts.

I know how you feel, Buddy.

Darwin was not happy as the conversation started. The tone in her voice told him she was letting him go. Her platitudes and pleas for understanding were a joke to him. She had broken a promise.

"We must be honest with each other, Darwin," she told him. "We don't have a great deal in common."

"What does commonality have to do with marriage?" he asked incredulously.

Savannah removed his ring and placed it back in the box he had given her. "What we have in common is critical to our beliefs as a couple and the glue that would hold us together when times get rough."

"You are not marrying me because you think I don't believe in that principle?"

Savannah touched his arm. "No. I am not marrying you because you don't believe in me."

Darwin stood, staring at her, trying to figure out what to say. He had nothing. She was right. Almost everything she thought or chose, he would question or correct her.

"I understand."

Was this a trick?

"I wish you the best, Savannah, but I have to know." He took a second before asking her. "Did you ever love me?"

She embraced him fully, with sincerity and with love said, "I still do and always will."

"You were just never *in* love with me?"

She shook her head no. There was no need to explain

that no matter how much she tried or believed they would eventually grow in love, it was never going to happen. *Darwin, you are an ass.* "I will give you back the money for the dress when I get to the bank after the holidays."

He placed a kiss on her forehead. "No need, keep it as a gift from me. I hate that I will never get to see you in that dress, but ..." His words trailed off.

This was unlike Darwin and Savannah was nervous, and even he sensed it. "I know, it is unlike me, but I honor my agreements."

Savannah's stomach lurched as she asked, "What agreement and with whom?"

"With Jesse," Darwin told her, as he put on his coat.

The vein in her right temple throbbed as she clenched her teeth, trying to sound far calmer than she was. "What agreement would that be, Darwin?"

"If you chose him, I wouldn't be a bitch about it," he told her as he slipped on his neck scarf.

"And if I had chosen you?" She wanted to know.

He slipped the ring into his coat pocket as he opened her front door. "He would let me keep my job."

And there it was.

Jesse understood Darwin far better than she ever had. He knew what was important to the man and sadly now, so did Savannah. However, the burgeoning question was what was essential to how she wanted to live her life.

Chapter Thirty-Two

It was the longest month of Savannah's life. She broke it off with Darwin on New Year's Eve so she could start the next day with a fresh year and a fresh perspective. He was snarky that she had chosen Jesse when she admitted, "I have not chosen him over you. I have chosen me."

That is what she told herself as she moped around the lab for three weeks trying to sort through her misguided notions about what truly went into a solid relationship. Her mother banned her from the house until she was able to find her smile, but it was Jerwane that helped her decide. "He loves you and you love him. You were at your best when you were seeing that big handy man."

"Jerwane, at one point I was convinced that I needed a man to take care of me, look after me, and make sure that I ate, had a roof over my head, and would be able to drive *that* car, have *that* house, and be a part of all the right social circles. After spending some time with Jesse, I realized I don't need that, but I am not sure what I need now, you know?"

Jerwane paused and took his little sister in his arms. He had spent a lifetime shielding her from the harshness of the world, including mean girls who wanted to pull her hair. He had sheltered her from nasty boys who wanted in her pants. Jerwane had even protected her when they had come home from school to find their father dead in his sleep. Savannah had stopped smiling after that and it wasn't until her time with Jesse that she had started laughing again. She walked around the world with eyes sharpened to every detail, yet her face registered nothing. To understand her, a person had to read her eyes. Jesse was able to do that and bring out a playful side in his sister.

"You need to be happy. I miss seeing you happy. I don't like you like this." He gulped at the bile rising in his throat as his mind formed the words he was about to say, "Call him and go get your molecule scrambling on, girl!"

She laughed, smushed his face, and picked up the phone.

He answered on the third ring, and she spoke soft words in the phone, "Are you ready to come home, Lost Boy?"

Jesse was smiling from ear to ear. "No, it is time to bring you to our home. Pack for a week and I will pick you and the cat up on Friday."

"Jesse?"

"Yes, Savannah."

"I've missed you."

"I've missed the hell out of you as well, my lovely."

On Friday evening, she and Thursday were packed and ready to go. Where they were going was uncertain, but she was starting a life with Jesse. Jerwane had agreed to move in and take over the payments of her condo, taking care of two birds with one stone. Jesse arrived at 6 pm sharp, still in work clothes and looking sexy as hell. *Do we have time for one before the road?*

"Hey, Science Girl," he greeted her, removing his gloves and wrapping his arms around her.

He smelled so good. Her body awoke and wanted to play. She grabbed her coat, but he was looking about the place, visually cataloguing what was in the condo.

"Before we leave this house, I have one question for you, Savannah." He lowered himself to one knee.

"I never got a chance to ask before. I had all of these speeches prepared, with cute catch phrases worked out, but in the end, all I want to know is, will you marry me?"

He held her left hand, toying with the ring he had given her months prior. His blue eyes were gazing up at hers, which were holding tears brimming at the rims.

"Yes. Yes, I will marry you."

He had not moved. His eyes were darting back and forth. *Was he stuck on the floor?*

"No, Savannah, I mean will you marry me, like next week? Darwin waited a year, but I am not going to do that. If you are going to marry me, I want it done next week."

"But what about the wedding?"

"You can plan the wedding for whenever you want, but Monday, I want to do the blood tests and on Wednesday or Thursday, hit the courthouse. You can have your pastor meet us or I can call mine, or we can use whichever one is milling about the courthouse."

He was serious. She stared into his unflinching blue eyes.

"Oh, my God, you are serious!"

"I am not getting up from here and we are not walking out that door until we settle this."

Savannah's head was spinning. "Okay. It's settled. Yes, I will marry you."

"When?" he asked.

"Next week is fine by me or would you like to fly off to Vegas and do it tomorrow?"

He stood up slowly. "No, next week is just fine." The softness in his eyes caressed her more gently than his hands ever did. "I love you, Savannah."

"I love you, too, Jesse." She wanted him right now, but he only kissed her briefly and collected her bag while she carried Thursday in the kitty case.

He had cleaned his truck, and he loaded them up and began the drive down I-65. Next week, she would be his wife.

They chatted briefly about the past month and she confessed she let Darwin go on New Year's Eve. Jesse understood her need to take the time to sort through the raw emotions, but it took three weeks for her to call.

"I needed to make sure. I am in love with you. I can't imagine my life without you and I knew that I wanted to give you pretty, smart children with exceptional taste in furniture."

He laughed and reached across the seat to hold her hand as he drove. His cell phone chirped and he pushed the button on the steering wheel, making the call come through the truck speakers.

"Hey, Big Bro, did you ask?" It was Mary Kate.

"I did."

"And?"

"She is sitting right here next to me, and we are headed home." Mary Kate squealed in delight.

"Oh my goodness, I am going to have a sister. Welcome to the family, Savannah!" The next words were a run-on sentence and Savannah mumbled in between the barrage of adjectives and expletives Mary Kate flung at her.

"Jesse," she said. "Savannah will need a household account with at least 20 so we can buy art for the all of those bare walls, and she has to get some new china. Savannah, I know a great place to get china at this outlet mall outside of Boaz. Get my number from Jesse and call me next week. I would love to sit down with you and your mama and help out wherever you need me to, Sis."

"It sounds great, Mary Kate," Savannah said and her soon to be sister-in-law squealed again.

"I'm hanging up on you, MK," Jesse said and clicked off the line.

China? Of all the things on her to-do list, buying china was not at the top. She was getting married next week. Before she could process her thoughts, his phone rang again. This time it was Ruth.

"Hey, Ma," he said.

"Did she say yes, Son? Big Sam is here with me."

"She did and put it on speaker so I can talk to you both," he said calmly as he maneuvered through Friday night traffic.

Savannah could hear her calling her husband, telling him the great news. "Sam we are going to having genius grandbabies."

Jesse cleared his throat, embarrassed, "Grandchildren are a few years away guys. We have time."

"Oh pshaw. When is the wedding?"

Jesse looked at Savannah. "I am thinking June."

Ruth yelled into the phone, "As long as it's inside. Mary Kate had a June wedding in our back yard in tent! It's way too warm in Alabama in June to be outside in a tent!"

Savannah stared at Jesse's profile and he seemed unfazed by any of it. "Ma, I'm driving." Big Sam yelled hello into the phone and Savannah smiled in the dark cabin of the truck as Thursday mewled from her lap. Savannah imagined the two of them sitting there yelling at the phone on the table.

"Savannah darling, get my number from Jesse and call me next week. Five months is not a lot of time. I would be happy to sit with you and your mama and lend a hand with whatever you need me to do, okay?"

"Thank you, Ruth," she said. It was nice that both she and May Kate had pretty much offered the same help. It was a refreshing change.

"Call me Mom, Savannah." The emotion could be heard through the phone.

"I will call you next week, Mom." Ruth began to blubber and Big Sam yelled in the phone. "I am hanging up now."

Savannah looked at Jesse. "Is Joe going to call next?"

"Doubtful, he'll just want to know when to show up and if there will be shrimp."

"Not in June, there won't be!" She laughed a bit but was shocked when her phone buzzed. *I'm not expecting any calls.*

She answered it tentatively. Jerwane's voice came through the phone, "Where you?"

"In the truck with Jesse," she told him.

"Put me on speaker." She hit the button. His voice boomed through the small speakers of her phone, "Where is the new facility, Mr. Rogers?"

Savannah looked confused. *What were they talking*

about? Why was he calling Jesse Mr. Rogers? What facility?

"Vestavia Hills, on Boulder Lake Circle," he said as he switched off of I-65 to I-459.

Jerwane had a few questions. "So, what do you like, football, boxing?"

Jesse's eyes stayed on the road. "I am a Falcons fan and will on occasion watch a prize fight, but it's not really my thing."

"What is your thing?"

"I like to make furniture and fish," Jesse told him.

Jerwane exhaled loudly, "Damn, you are so white!"

Jesse glanced over at her and she shrugged, *What can I say to that?*

"Ahhh, Jerwane, is everything okay?"

"Yeah, Button Nose. Are you sure about this?"

"I am," she said softly. "Are you ready to hand me over to him?"

"I'm okay with it and I guess I am going to have to learn to fish. I am not making any furniture though, but I may watch on occasion." Jerwane got quiet, not certain if the next part should be on speaker or not, but he wanted Jesse to hear, "Hey, Button Nose?"

"Yes?"

"I love you, you know that right?"

"I love you, too, Jerwane." She hung up.

Jesse turned down Liberty Parkway, then onto Sicard Hollow Road and made a left onto Lake Colony Way. "Button Nose, huh?"

"Hush," she told him wagging her finger in warning to never use that pet name with her. "And I will never find my way back up here."

"It's programmed into the GPS."

There was a moment of silence. Then she gazed out the side window, speaking modestly, "Next week I am going to be your wife."

She did not realize he heard her until he responded, "In my mind you have been my wife since you packed my lunch and put apple pie in my tool box. Next week we just make official."

They entered Vestavia Hills and pulled up to a relatively new two-story brick home. Jesse pulled around back to a four-car garage and steered the truck up to the rear sunroom. He opened her door and helped her out with the cat and guided her into the back door.

The housekeeper came out to greet them. Jesse handed the matronly Hispanic woman the cat and the bag as he turned to scoop Savannah up in his arms to carry her over the threshold. They stepped into an immaculate kitchen with state-of-the- art appliances. "Jesse, where are we?" she asked.

"You are home, my lovely. This is our house."

Chapter Thirty - Three

Savannah was taken aback. This was a very large house in Vestavia Hills. She was standing in a kitchen any woman would be proud to have, next to a man that she truly loved. She watched the housekeeper unpack Thursday and give her some food and water. Jesse slipped his hand into hers after the housekeeper disappeared around the corner.

"Let me show you our home," he told her, pulling at her arm. Savannah didn't budge.

"What's wrong, Savannah?"

"I have not seen you or touched you in a month. The tour can wait. There is only one room I am interested in seeing."

Jesse exhaled a sigh of relief. "Thank Heavens, because I am so backed up, I am having headaches!" He told her to follow him as he made his way through the kitchen, across the foyer, and up the stairs. The master bedroom sat in the rear of the house on the second floor at the end of the hallway. As they walked down the hallway, a curved banister overlooked the formal living room. All of the walls in the home were beige with dark brown hardwood floors. Savannah shook her head. She would think about color schemes and bright rugs later. Right now, her mind was on Jesse.

"I've had an easy day, but if you want to shower first to wash the day away, I can hold on a little while longer," he said to her as she reached for the belt buckle on his khakis, pushing him toward the bed. She unfastened his pants and reached inside to grab the goods. "Or, maybe not ..." His words were lost as he felt her tongue flick across the head of his rapidly hardening interest.

Think, Jesse, focus. "The great thing is, sweetheart, we get to be as loud and as messy as we want." He sucked in his breath when she took him in her mouth.

"Good Lord! You keep that up and I am going to get messy on your face!" He tried to pull away, but she wouldn't let him. He urged her again to stop. "Savannah, it's been a month, I only have so much resolve ... ooooh, that feels amazing." He threw back his head back onto the bed, enjoying the pleasure she was bringing him.

Enough.

"Clothes off, now!"

Savannah struggled to her feet while Jesse tugged at her clothes, his pants still around his ankles. He reached under her skirt and pulled at whatever he felt, the stringed thong giving way in his hand. Their shoes had been left in the mudroom by the door and Jesse reached for her right leg, lifting her up onto the bed, aiming for her sweet spot. He pressed his hips upward, experiencing her warmth. *Not enough.*

"Come on, Baby," he told her as he grabbed her by the hips, gently lifting her up then lowering her hips over his throbbing need until he had completely impaled her upon him. Her arms wrapped tightly about his neck, her breasts smashed into his chest, and he jostled her up and down. *Still not enough.*

Jesse pulled at her hips as he tried to create a rhythm, but they were both in hurry, not working together in the king sized bed. He asked her to stop, while rolling her to her back and disconnecting them. He kicked off his pants then pulled off her skirt. "Savannah, Savannah, my sweet Science Girl, my love, my wife," he whispered in her ear as he slowly entered her and they began to move together.

It no longer embarrassed her to meet her climax so soon. "Oh, Jesse," she cried out as she began her ascent. He was not far behind her as they collapsed in a tangle of legs and clothing, holding each other, basking in the afterglow of their lovemaking.

Somewhere in the middle of the night, they found their way back to the kitchen. Theresa, the housekeeper, had cooked a ham for dinner and Savannah found some rolls in the pantry and made sliders for them to nosh on before they returned to the bedroom for a second round.

"Jesse, I love you," she said as she settled into his arms and drifted off to sleep.

"I love you back, Science Girl" He kissed the top of her head and experienced a newfound peace as he drifted off to his own private Neverland.

Savannah awoke to an empty bed. Turning slowly, she saw the morning sun shining brightly into the room, even for late January. She sat up in the bed and took stock of the bedroom. The king sized bed did not have a headboard, only an ecru colored Matelassé covering for bedding, and two king sized pillow. The walls were beige, there were no rugs on the floor and outside of a gentleman's chest of 15 drawers and a mirrored dresser, the room was bare.

The floors were not cold as she tiptoed to the bathroom. The fireplace that resided in the wall had been lit, emanating warmth into the bedroom as well as the bathroom, a bathroom that bordered on amazing! It boasted two separate vanities, with hers having an overstuffed dressing chair. There was natural light from the window and she even had her own private water closet. Jesse had his own as well. *Well, now don't that beat all?* The oversized Jacuzzi tub sat in the middle of the bathroom, dividing her side from his with the shower next to the tub.

Savannah showered quickly and dressed, placing her items in the dresser. To the left of the bed were two doors; she figured these were closets. She opened the one on the left, and his scent wafted out, filling her nostrils and igniting her hormones. The shirts were lined up by color, then by sleeve length. Almost every one had the Montgomery Construction logo. The back of the closet held his shoes, all six pairs including the sandals she had purchased for him. The right side of the closet held a few suits, some ties, and slacks in three colors: khaki, blue, and black. *Okay, then.*

She closed the door and went to the other closet. Her breath caught. She could almost hear the angels singing as she noticed the lingerie chest, a full-length mirror, a settee, a tea table, and a rack from ceiling to floor for shoes! Savannah pinched herself to make sure it was real. The rumbling of her tummy halted her fantasy romp through closet heaven and shoe racks than ran to the ceiling.

As she made her way down the hall, there were three empty bedrooms on the master bedroom floor. She peered inside the first, which was mid-sized – her bedroom furniture would go in here. The second room she peeked in was slightly smaller. Her guest room furniture could go here. But near the stairwell was another set of stairs that went up. She followed the stairs to an empty space that would be ideal for a children's play area. It must have been what Jesse had in mind as well, as an antique tricycle sat in the corner of the room. *Okay, four bedrooms upstairs with a bonus room.*

Slowly, she went to her starting point in the upstairs hallway and looked over the balcony into the formal living room. It was empty, but the fireplace was beautiful, with large hand set stones surrounding it over what appeared to be a hand carved wooden mantle. Unlike the gas burning one in the bedroom, this one burned wood. *Great for winter storms and power outages.*

The formal dining room held a wooden table that would easily seat ten, but there were no chairs. She eyed the wood closely, grinning from ear to ear when she realized Jesse had made the table. Burned into the wood was a logo featuring a large O, with cursive JM in the center. Off the side of the dining room was an office filled with papers, blue prints, and two overstuffed chairs. *This was his space.*

Savannah walked back through the dining room and headed toward the other side of the house, to the kitchen. She entered from the other side, versus the way they had come up the stairs last night and found herself in a humongous great room, with another wood burning fireplace and walls that were also beige. The room held no furniture. By her calculations, the house in total was easily 4,500 square feet. *It is going to take me five years of penny-pinching just to furnish this place.*

In the kitchen was a small table with two chairs. The

legs were very similar to the dining room table and Savannah peered underneath the table to look for his logo. *It is there, as well as on the chairs.* She heard someone clear their throat and popped up on her feet to see an older white man standing there. *Relative?*

"Good morning there, Mrs. Montgomery, I hope you didn't mind me helping myself to coffee. Jesse will be back inside in a minute."

Savannah looked over her shoulder to see if anyone was standing behind her. *Mrs. Montgomery?* She played it cool. "No problem, I think I will grab a cup myself. And may I ask who you are?"

"I'm Jeb. Jeb Montgomery, I'm Jesse's uncle. I guess I'm yours too, or will be once you to make it official. Big Sam is my brother."

Her eyebrows went up. "Pleasure to meet you, Jeb, and please call me Savannah."

Savannah's hands shook as she poured her coffee. Jesse was a Montgomery of Montgomery Construction. She thought about Darwin's words, *"He would let me keep my job."*

Anger coursed through her as she rifled through their conversations. He had lied to her and told her he didn't make six figures, remembering his words, *but between your new raise and what I make, we would do okay.*

She wasn't sure how okay he was going to be when he walked through that back door. *Why did he lie to me? And why do I not ask for people's last names?*

Chapter Thirty - Four

Jesse entered the backdoor and saw her sitting at the table with Uncle Jeb. "Good morning, my lovely," he said as he bent down to kiss her good morning.

Savannah rose and fetched a cup. "Let me pour you some coffee, Mr. Montgomery. Uncle Jeb, would you like to join us for breakfast?"

Jesse's eyes were wide with her realization. He was planning to tell her this morning, but Jeb had shown up earlier than expected.

Uncle Jeb declined on breakfast. "I am just here to get the keys to your place so I can get the movers in a get everything over here this weekend and you will be ready to rock and roll on Monday." Savannah retrieved her keys from her purse and passed them over to Uncle Jeb.

"Great, we should have everything here at least by 4 pm, so all you have to do is point to where you want it." Jesse gave the man a hug as he took his cup of coffee and headed out the backdoor, nodding his head to Savannah.

At this point, a serious conversation was needed with her husband to be.

"We'll see you at four, and it was a pleasure meeting you," she told him as she retrieved eggs from the fridge, along with some turkey bacon, and started breakfast.

Uncle Jeb waved goodbye and Jesse knew in the way she beat the eggs that she was madder than a wet cat. Thursday made an appearance, rubbing against her legs begging for food. Jesse picked up the little ball of fur and set out some food and fresh water for her.

Savannah made the plates and set them on the table, pushing Jesse to ask, "Is this our first fight and if so, afterwards can we have some messy makeup sex?"

"How could you not tell me you were Montgomery Construction? Isn't that a detail I needed to know?"

"Nope, it wasn't relevant until now," he told her after he blessed the food and started eating.

Jesse explained again that it was a family-run business and after the conference, he thought she knew. He further described his role in the company as a worker, moving his way through the ranks by earning every job title he had sported. "Orison is my middle name, so the workers would not see me as the company, but as their boss."

"Your middle name means truth and you couldn't tell me you run Montgomery Construction?"

"Thanks to you, I do now. I got a promotion recently," he told her as he sipped his coffee. Jesse explained at each convention, it was his job, along with Big Sam, Jeb, and Bart to bring in new business. "Taking over the reins from Big Sam was between me and my cousin Bart, Jeb's son."

Did I meet Bart?

"We both have the same credentials, same training, and the same years in the company, but with one difference."

"What is that?"

"On that Friday and Saturday night in Colorado, somehow, and I don't know what you said to those men, but you got me four new contracts. Those four contracts made me president of Montgomery Construction."

Savannah sat at the table, staring at him. "What do you expect from me as your wife, Jesse, to do more of the same?"

"I expect you to love me. As you told my brother, your job is to make me forget the office, fortify me so I can go back each day and do the job. My job as your husband is to keep you happy and give you the things you want to keep you satisfied. *We* raise some kids, and they go off to college at Alabama." He lowered his head in reverence as he said, "Crimson Tide ... and grow old together."

"You make it seem so simple, but you lied to me."

"Tell me what I lied to you about, Savannah?"

Her hands flew in the air, pointing around the house, the room. "This! You. What is this? Did you buy this house for us?"

"No. I bought this house for me. It just happens to be in an area you wanted to live in, which further proves my point about us belonging together."

She wasn't letting it go, asking through tight lips, "When did you buy the house?"

"Two years ago. Bart's side of the business does the high end residential. This is a Montgomery Construction home. Actually, Uncle Jeb built this and the framework, along with the garage. I got it at half the cost and spent the last two years finishing the interior, which is why it is not furnished and all the walls are that boring beige. I will leave the decorating to you."

"What did you specialize in?" She was irritated that she had not asked these questions months ago, "And why is Uncle Jeb moving me?"

Jesse was trying to answer all of her questions, but she was angry and when she was mad, it was like sitting through a session of Crossfire. "I specialize in building residential communities, townhomes, condos, like the one you lived in. I lived in one of the units onsite in your complex while we finished up before moving on to the Riverchase Project. Uncle Jeb's brother-in-law owns a moving company."

He poured them both more coffee as he cleared their plates and started some dishwater. "My cousin Paul and his dad Mathew head up the commercial side of the business. There wasn't a great deal of commercial business, which is why Paul was not in the running for President. However, the contract you helped me land is making the commercial arm a nice profit generator." He paused for a minute. "Hey, what does my brother-in-law do for living? The subject has never come up."

"Jerwane is a pediatric physical therapist," Savannah mumbled.

Jesse looked perplexed, "That is not something I would have imagined a big guy like your brother doing." *Color me surprised, I thought he was a night-club bouncer.*

She was still uncertain of what she had signed up for, but he had been smarter than her and got her to accept his proposal before all of this was sprung upon her. "Jesse, what does this mean for us, especially with me being the President's wife?"

He explained that she needed to find a charity she was passionate about, transition out his mother's cause, or continue it, whichever was her preference. "On occasion, we will have some clients over for dinner, one of which will be Bob Walker from Walker Industries. We got the contract to build his new manufacturing plant, along with two other commercial deals and a new residential community in Mississippi, from one of those women who were feeling you up in the bathroom with my sister."

Jesse waggled his eyebrows.

"Savannah, I never thought I could do the job and never wanted it, but you convinced me I could do anything. So, I stepped up so I could give you all the things you said you needed to be happy."

Savannah leaned her face into her hands. "Jesse, having and sharing a life with you is enough to make me happy. Not only have I learned what is important, I also gained a clearer understanding of who I am." She got quiet and looked at the bare pantries. "How am I supposed to furnish this house? How are we going to afford this?"

He pulled her up from the table and wrapped his arms around her waist. "Savannah, with each contract I bring in, I get 10% off the top. Since you were the one to help me get those four, I will give half of my commissions to my wife. This gives you a nice operating budget for the household. I will pay the mortgage and utilities and you take care of insurance, food, and house shit."

"You are okay with letting me decorate the house without your input?" She pulled back and looked up at him.

"I can never think of a day or a time when I want to look at fabric swatches, pick china patterns, or determine if a painting *moves me*. But if you want my input, you got it."

The ease with which they talked had dissipated her anger. "But, my office is off limits to you and your decorating touch. And ..." he kissed her nose. "... I will make one request."

"And what would that be, husband?"

"The family room furniture should be a comfortable

sectional and I want a big daddy chair that reclines and vibrates. Matter of fact, make it two, for when your brother or my Dad comes over."

Savannah had relaxed a bit, but she didn't have any way to get around, and she thought that maybe they would go and get her car later. "Any other surprises, Mr. Montgomery?"

He lowered his head and kissed her thoroughly. "Well, yeah, there are three."

"Surprises?"

Jesse slipped his hand in hers, grabbed her coat from the rack, and pulled her out the patio door to the side of the house and a small freestanding building. He opened the door of the cottage to reveal a full-fledged workshop for furniture- making. "Of course, you will have to make your own logo to go on your stuff." Savannah was choked up with emotion. She loved the workshop. *Maybe I can make most of the pieces for the house.*

"You have full access to the shop. Just put my tools back where you found them and we will be okay," he told her as he pulled her by the hand to the garage. "The other things I was working on this week were these." He opened the first garage door to reveal a shiny blue 4-door Chevy S-10.

"I figured you would need something to drive to pick up wood and supplies and stuff."

Savannah hugged him tightly. It was the most adorable truck, but the second garage door went up, as he told her with pride, "Because I knew you couldn't haul wood in this."

Her hands flew to her face as she stared at an upgrade to her dream car. It was a four door Sapphire Gray

Metallic E-class, with a big red bow on the hood. The pink front license plate had an unraveling DNA strand that almost matched her lunch bag. *Detailed.*

"I didn't fit too well in the C-Class and then I thought about the kids in a few years and knew you needed more room." She threw her arms around his neck, kissing him before moving over to look closer at her new car. "I don't know how we are going to afford all of this." Her fingers trailed over the sleek lines of her new baby.

"Don't worry. I paid for those out of your cut of the commission. The truck isn't new, but the car is. The title will arrive in the next few weeks." He started to laugh as she swatted at his arm.

"If we spend wisely, save, and invest, you will never have to worry about being hungry." He watched her touch the car as if it were going to disappear if she rubbed it too hard. It had an applied-for vanity plate that read TNKRBEL2. She loved it, but what was number one if her car was two?

It was a four-car garage. "What is behind the other two doors?" Door number three held Jesse's six year old Cherokee and behind door number four was a shiny black Camaro, sitting proudly on shiny custom rims with yellow and red flames beginning at the car's nose and spreading down the side of the vehicle.

Savannah yelled like she was seeing and old friend, "Tinkerbell!!!!!"

A proud Jesse was grinning like a school kid who just made it to third base on a second date. "Does she run? Can we take her out for a drive? How fast does she go?"

He held up his hands to slow her down and she tried to open the doors. *She wasn't that excited about her own vehicles.* Jesse was somewhat amused until she asked the deal-breaking question, "Baby, can I drive her?"

He did not hold his tongue. "I don't know if I love you that much!"

"You are supposed to love me no matter what, Jesse Montgomery."

He shook his head. "No, Science Girl, that is Jesus, not me!" They stood in the drive in front of the garages, laughing at each other. "I will take you out for a ride in her. Grab those keys from the key box."

He pressed the fob once and unlocked the doors. When he pressed it again, the engine started. Savannah slid into the passenger seat like it was their first date. There was so much more to learn about her husband. Next on her list was his music choice.

"I know this is a weird question and a fine time to ask almost a year later, but what type of music do you like?"

"What else? Southern Rock!" He revved Tinkerbelle's engine, licked his two fingers and touched the gearshift, let up off the clutch, and eased her out of the garage. He pressed the third button on the fob and all the garage doors came down. As Skynyrd blasted from the radio, they chugged down the road, softly through residential streets. He rubbed the dashboard, telling Tinkerbell, "Not yet, my lovely."

When they hit the open road, he let up on the clutch, pressed the gas, and shifted the gear, and the car responded by opening up her engines and giving Jesse everything she had. Savannah knew that feeling well. She responded the same way each time he touched her.

Thursdays in Savannah

Epilogue

Hey there, I am glad you stayed and heard me out. I know, I had a lot of misconceived notions about life, love, and so much more. Jesse was very patient and waited for me to make my own decision, and I am thankful that it was the right one for both of us. We have been married for four years.

The wedding was small, intimate, and at my family's church. I made sure the ushers took care of the seating so the ceremony didn't look like a school board meeting on integration. I was also right about the dress. It was stunning once I added the touches to it with decorative pearls and beads. The veil was cathedral length in shimmering white tulle with sewn-in pearls. The blusher was interlaced with live baby's breath and the whole thing was trimmed in this beautiful lace that my grandmother had given my mom. Not meaning to brag, but I really looked beautiful. I was so stunning that when my brother lifted the veil, Jesse began kissing me before the pastor even started the ceremony. My husband is funny.

As president of Montgomery Construction, Jesse was able to make some much- needed changes in the organizational structure by pooling the resources of the divisions. If things were slow on the commercial side, but booming in multi-dwelling units, he began a cross-training program so every employee and worker could have a forty-hour work week. Lucky thing he did. The commercial side of the business picked up and

Montgomery Construction is more profitable than it had ever been. Everything worked out well, even for Darwin, who did so great on the Riverchase Project that Jesse hired him as a full time architect. He now is in charge of the custom home design department.

Big Sam and Ruth retired, and with my percentage from the contracts I helped Jesse bring in each year at the conferences, I was able to retire my mother as well. She still works, but her new job is more a labor of love that allows her to walk to work. Darwin designed a custom cottage for her that Jesse had built on one of the back acres of the property. For my mother, the idea of having a nanny was out of the question, and right before I gave birth to our first child, she moved into her new home. She lives close, but still has her own drive, her own address, and her own privacy.

"Mommiiieeeeeee!"

Excuse me for a minute. Sahara, my mother's new job, is calling me. This little girl is two going on twenty-five and absolutely spoiled rotten. Between Ruth, Jerwane, and Big Sam, she has them all wrapped around her cute little finger, and her father is worse. After her daddy tells her all of the magical stories of special worlds, she loves to don her favorite outfit, the fairy suit that sports pink fairy wings. Trying to leave the house without those things attached to her back is another story altogether. Although I am biased, because she's mine, that child is so adorable. Sahara is beautiful, with creamy café au lait skin, giant hazel eyes which sparkle when she smiles, two little chubby cherub cheeks, and the dark curly hair that always seems to be a mess.

"Mommmmmiieee, Uncle J got fish!" Let me go and see

what this little girl is screaming about from the back door.

Oh, Jesse and Jerwane have just returned from fishing and my brother has a string of stinky fish he is going to insist upon cleaning in my kitchen sink. Yes, the two of them are best buds now, especially after Jesse surprised him for his birthday a few years ago. Jerwane was beside himself when Jesse showed him the plane tickets to Vegas. As strong as my brother is, I have never seen him cry, not even at our father's funeral, but he cried like a six-year-old girl when my husband presented him the tickets to see Floyd Mayweather fight at the MGM Grand on that Vegas trip. Jesse got him the V.I.P. treatment. He even called in a few favors and Jerwane got to meet Pretty Boy Floyd in person. I'm not sure what else happened on that trip, but Jerwane came back with a busted lip and Jesse had Sahara tattooed across his heart and Savannah tattooed across his butt cheek. Every now and then, they share a look and a sly smirk. Well, what happens in Vegas... at least they both came back happy.

As for me, I am happier than I have ever been. I smile all the time and even tell a few jokes. They are science jokes, but hey, I've lightened up a lot. It took a year for me to grow up and understand that the things I thought were necessary for a good life were not, sharing your life with someone who makes you happy is important. Sharing your life with someone who appreciates you for who you are is even more imperative. Jesse makes me happy and I love our life together.

I can hear the pitter-patter of Sahara's little feet coming this way and I know what she wants. It is Saturday. Each Saturday afternoon is her time with Daddy. If it is not tea parties or something else, he straps her into the back seat for an afternoon drive in Tinkerbell. Each time he revs the engine, Sahara giggles like it is the greatest thing in the world. Truth be told, so do I.

"Mommy, I called you," Sahara tells me as she rounds the corner.

"Sweetie, Mommy is moving a little slower these days," I tell her as I slowly try to stand.

"...because of Daniel?" She wants to know as she places her tiny hands upon my enormous belly.

"Yes, Sahara. Daniel is getting too big to stay inside of Mommy's tummy much longer."

I am smiling as she places her ear to my stomach, attempting to hear Daniel who unfortunately, becomes very active each time he hears his sister's voice.

"Is he done yet, Mommy? Is he ready to come out of there?"

It takes a little effort, but I squat down to give her a juicy wet kiss on the cheek, "Not yet, my lovely, but soon."

-Fin-

Smile for the camera Sahara...

COMING FALL 2014

The Davonshire Series

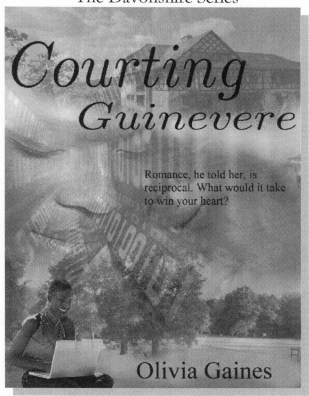

ABOUT THE AUTHOR

Olivia Gaines is the author of numerous best selling novellas and books including Two Nights in Vegas, A Few More Nights, and have had several number one best sellers with The Blakemore Files including Being Mrs. Blakemore and Shopping with Mrs. Blakemore.

She lives in Augusta, GA with her husband, son and snotty cat, Katness Evermean.

Connect with Olivia on her FaceBook page at http://on.fb.me/1eorEAr or her website at http://oliviagaines.com.

Made in the USA
Charleston, SC
09 August 2014